DOWN BOUND TRAIN

Down Bound Train

by BILL GARNETT

DOUBLEDAY & COMPANY, INC., GARDEN CITY, NEW YORK
1973

ISBN: 0-385-01820-7
Library of Congress Catalog Card Number 72–92402
Copyright © 1973 by Bill Garnett
All Rights Reserved
Printed in the United States of America
First Edition

"It's easy to go down to Hell.
Night and day its sad gates stand wide.
But to call back your steps and escape to the upper air,
This is a toil, this a task."

Vergil

DOWN BOUND TRAIN

CHAPTER 1

Heaven.

The church was a vision of it realised in stone. The echoes down cool grey cloisters whispered peace; soft light prismed from stained-glass windows of celestial sunrise; the very reach of tall Gothic arches was the straining up of wings to God.

In such a setting, the presence of the man who now turned from the High Altar and spread out thigh-thick arms in blessing seemed a grotesque and tasteless mistake.

Even the magnificence of his rich ecclesiastical vestments did not lessen his ugliness—and could the Reverend Sullivan Staymore have seen himself through the eyes of the four hundred dark-suited boys who knelt in the church before him, that morning of September the twenty-third, even he might have been awed.

He was six feet four inches tall and the pillars and arches around him did not diminish his stature. He was grotesquely fat, weighing nearly three hundred pounds. His small, close-shaven head was perfectly round and sat like a pallid cannon-ball on his huge oval body—without a sign of a neck. His nose was a length of pipe. His eyes were pellets behind thick spectacles. As always he was imperfectly shaven and now, near the conclusion of Mass, the sweat which welled from his head had found channels through his closely bristled cheeks down to his multiple chins.

He let his little eyes flicker down the nave of the church to the boys who knelt for his blessing. They were wretches every one of them, he thought. No one needed the benediction of Almighty God more than they.

"Go in peace. The Mass is ended."

"Thanks be to God."

These rich and pampered children had many things to be thankful for, the Reverend Sullivan considered as he turned to complete the Mass. Not the least of them that they had him to help them on the path to salvation. The wisdom of the Lord was everywhere you looked. And nowhere more manifest to the Reverend Sullivan's eyes than in the fact that God had seen fit to appoint him headmaster of this mighty Catholic boarding school for the last ten years.

He wobbled from the altar into the sacristy and began to wrestle out of his vestments. As he did so, he could hear the sounds of the boys leaving church. It disgusted him how much quicker they always went out than came in. He imagined he knew their thoughts precisely: dismissive of the miraculous sacrament at which they had just participated, their horrible minds would be on breakfast or some other worthless pleasure that the day held in store.

But the Reverend Sullivan Staymore was wrong.

For in the mind of at least one of the uniformed boys who filed in swift silence down the wood-panelled corridors towards the dining hall, there was no pleasure at all.

There was fear.

Evelyn Price was fourteen. He'd been at the school a year and throughout that time fear had been his relentless companion. It had fled beside him on the games field; waited shivering with him in cold passageways for beatings that would come in the night. Most of all, it had crystallised and centered itself in the towering omnipresence of the Reverend Sullivan Staymore. Headmaster. Priest who had just said Holy Mass.

Evelyn milled into the dining hall with the other boys and stood in silence by a table waiting for grace. A single thought obsessed him. A prefect had told him the headmaster wanted to see him after breakfast. But why? What had he done?

Evelyn didn't hear grace and sat down to breakfast in a daze. His blond healthy features were pale. A plate of cereal was passed down the table to him. He looked at it and felt sick. What could he have done wrong this time? Surely Staymore wouldn't flog him straight after breakfast? Maybe there was news from home. In which case, it would have to be bad. Dear God, don't let Mum and Dad have been killed in a car crash, he prayed in his mind. No, it couldn't be that. Perhaps someone had just reported him for something. He had walked out of a masters-only door the day before yesterday. That must be it. He was only going to get beaten again.

He started to eat his cereal with a feeling that was almost relief. At which point the Reverend Sullivan Staymore entered the hall and sat down at the high table to break his own fast.

"Morning, sir!" the six prefects who shared the table with him exclaimed in unison as he sat.

"Good morning, gentlemen," he replied and began to eat. "Gentlemen" was hardly the word, he thought, forking food swiftly to his mouth. Still, these six youths were the pick of the school. Each and every one had been moulded at his hands. Now they sat in respectful silence as he finished his first course. The headmaster, they knew, did not appreciate distractions while he ate.

As always the hall is bedlam, Staymore fumed inwardly, pushing away his finished first course. He'd contemplated having silence imposed on all meals, but had decided it was preferable to have the evil children blabbing here—where their conversations could at least be overheard and any improprieties reported to him.

"I told Price you wanted to see him after breakfast, sir," the prefect on his right cut in on his thoughts.

"Ah!" Staymore said, turning his head to stare at the boy. He was seventeen. Antiseptic, instantly obedient. He came to Mass each morning without fail—even on the days when attendance was voluntary. He was a perfect choice for a prefect. A good-looking lad, too, Staymore reflected. Curly, cherubic blond hair, skin as fair and pure as an altar cloth . . .

Staymore checked himself with a feeling of anger. Living in an exclusively male community, there were dangers in this form of thought. He silently asked God's forgiveness.

"There's something else I feel I should mention, sir," the prefect went on.

"Yes, my dear?"

"On the subject of Price, sir—I saw him walking down a corridor last night. And he had his hands in his pockets. For at least a minute."

"Did he now? Disgusting child!" Staymore smiled. He liked to smile occasionally, unexpectedly. It always interested him how other people stopped smiling when he did.

"Will you be coming to the match this weekend, sir?" This was another prefect, leading light of the football team.

"I fear not. The Holy Father has summoned me to attend the Ecumenical Conference in Rome. Doubtless, though, you will win despite my absence."

"Yes, sir!" the boy replied enthusiastically. For the headmaster was not known to be gentle to those who lost.

"See that you do," Staymore replied severely. He gave himself to his second course. All sound at his table abruptly stopped.

Evelyn Price wasn't speaking either. But where he sat the conversation was loud around him.

"We'll smash 'em!"

"They won't score at all!"

12

"I'm not so sure. They've got a pretty tough side—and no one's beaten them yet."

"*We* will."

"I dunno . . ."

Evelyn hated football and stopped listening. What did it matter who won the lousy match anyway? It did matter, though, what Staymore was going to do to him after breakfast. It mattered more than anything in the world.

And now breakfast was ending. People were getting up and drifting out of the refectory. Evelyn sneaked a look at the high table. Staymore was there still, gorging himself. He'd spilt egg on his habit and hardly bothered to mop it up. As Evelyn stared at him, the fear he felt intensified till it seemed his stomach was turned to fluid which at any moment would drain irreplaceably from his body.

It was very hard indeed to think of that hideously ugly man as a holy Catholic priest.

Evelyn looked away. The hall was emptying fast. There wasn't any point in putting it off anymore. He forced himself to stand. And as best he could, he sauntered out.

Staymore saw him go. His chins quivered a little with anger and his tiny eyes screwed into the folds of his face. Little brat, he thought, he knew he was coming for a flogging, yet he strutted round as if he owned the place. It was time he was taught a lesson.

Staymore pushed back his plate, pushed himself to his feet. The table bent as he leaned on it.

"Tell Price I want him now. *Now!*" he hissed at a prefect. Then swung away.

He was still seething when he reached his study and sank into the sturdy swivel-chair behind his desk. He knew Price's type. He'd seen them often enough before. They thought they were superior; that they couldn't be made to knuckle down. Staymore's eyes went to the canes that stood in a stand by the window. By the holy wounds of Jesus, he'd show him! He would beat the brat till he bled.

But then he remembered that he'd have to be restrained.

He'd been too enthusiastic with a caning once before. The boy had been hospitalised and there'd nearly been an unpleasant enquiry. The sort of thing that could give a school a bad name and bring cries of "sadism" from every snivelling left-wing newspaper in the country. Yes, he would have to be more careful this time. He consoled himself with the thought that it didn't really matter.

There were other ways to break a boy.

He heard footsteps coming down the corridor. They seemed steady and confident. This would be Price. With surprising speed for a man of his bulk, the Reverend Sullivan Staymore leaned across his desk and flicked a switch on a control panel. It worked a light outside his door which would now read "engaged." Let him wait—and worry, thought Staymore, relaxing back in his chair.

And he picked up and opened his *Times*.

Outside in the teak-panelled passageway, Evelyn stopped before the headmaster's door. The closed study door with the impersonal sign above it. He looked at it. And, as he did so, fear cloaked itself around him and squeezed till the sweat wrung out on his palms and his stomach twisted into a rag. He had gone over the possibilities for the summons so many times now that his mind was numb. Fear was his being. He could do and think of nothing. Automatically, without even knowing he was doing it, he began to whistle, shrill and feeble as he waited.

Inside the study, Staymore heard the sound. It cut through his concentration on the newspaper and he put it down with a scowl. Everything about the boy was wrong. He should have been out there quaking, pacing a little perhaps, but his eyes never leaving the door. Instead he was merrily whistling—the damned impertinence!

Staymore heaved his legs up onto the desk, thoughtfully pressed his sausage-thick fingers together in front of his mouth. Absent-mindedly he began to chew on a finger-nail. He knew only too well what it felt like to stand outside that door.

Thirty-five years ago, he had stood there himself.

That Staymore was once a pupil where he was now head-

14

master was unknown to any of the boys now at the school—
and he intended to keep it that way. For his school-days had
been a period of ceaseless humiliation. A gangly, unco-ordinated child whose intensity and physical weakness made him
the butt of every bully's humour, he was relentlessly persecuted.
Now, of course, he was thankful for it. For his character had
been formed in pain. And it was pain he knew that paved the
path to God.

Still . . . it wouldn't do to have the children know.

Staymore looked at the Parker pen on his desk. They had
stuck pen-nibs into him in the classrooms, he remembered. They
had stripped off his trousers in the locker-room and plastered
him with boot polish. They had made him aware of the vileness
that is every child and man.

He had grown possessed with a determination to destroy it.

It had made him go into the Church. It had led him back to
this, his old school. It had finally brought him to the headmaster-
ship. Here the battle had begun. For, though he recognised that
each and every child in his care was the direct progeny and tool
of Satan, their evil took many forms and in his crusade against
it, he had to be ceaselessly vigilant in searching and stamping
it out. The Devil's ways were manifold and devious indeed.

Price, for example, was an instance of Satan's subtlety. The
child betrayed none of the more obvious traits of the adolescent.
As yet, Staymore had been unable to find him in cheating,
lying, stealing, drinking, smoking, bullying, drug-taking—any
of the usual things. But he knew beyond any doubt that filled
with sin the child must be: his very happiness proved it. And
before he left for Rome, he intended to find out exactly what
the sin was.

Which was why Price was here.

Staymore swung down his legs from the desk, got up and went
to a crucifix that hung on a wall. He knelt before it. Dear God,
he prayed, help me to root out the wickedness in this child—
and smash it. Then he got up, went back to his desk, folded the
newspaper and placed it in a drawer. He turned off the engaged
sign outside his door.

Evelyn Price saw the sign go out. It seemed like the floor lurched beneath him. His mouth dropped open and his legs went to water. Oh God, he prayed, don't let whatever's coming be too bad. Not more than I can take. Then he shook himself; squared back his shoulders; took a deep breath. And knocked on the door.

"Come!" Staymore called. And wondering if he'd ever be able to walk out again, Evelyn walked in.

Staymore was standing, back to the door, by a window near the end of the room. To Evelyn, who was hardly five feet tall, he appeared a towering shape with his black priest's robes seeming to all but frighten out the light from the window. He did not look round as Evelyn came in, shut the door, stood waiting uncertainly by it. Nor did he speak.

After the silence had become more than Evelyn could stand, he moved into the room a little way.

"Y-you sent for me, sir?" he stammered.

Staymore did not reply. But then one of the hands that was clasped behind his back opened and an immense forefinger summoned Evelyn to come nearer. Evelyn watched the thick blotchy thing as it curled and beckoned. Reluctantly he went and stood by Staymore's side at the window, uncertain if that was what he was meant to do.

Then, to his horror, and still without looking at him, Staymore reached out a massive arm and curled it round his shoulders and drew Evelyn close to his side.

"What do you see out of this window, my child?" Staymore asked. The question threw Evelyn into panic. There was a quadrangle, statue, school buildings, church, boys. "Um . . ." was all he could manage to reply.

"Don't um, boy!" Staymore told him softly. "You know what you see. You see the statue of the Blessed Virgin—who is the mother of us all."

"Yes, sir."

Evelyn stole a glance up from under his headmaster's arm at his face. It was bristly and sweaty and behind their thick glasses the priest's small eyes had screwed to snakes-tongues in a frown.

16

Evelyn shuddered as he realised that already he must have said something wrong.

"What does the statue tell you, Price?"

"Uh—I—I don't know, sir."

Staymore sighed. He took his arm from Evelyn's shoulder and moved away to his desk. Evelyn moved to face him.

"It makes me think of—it reminds me of the Virgin Mary, sir!" he tried in desperation.

Staymore sat down behind his desk and looked at him impassively for a moment without replying. Then he said: "You're an evil little boy, Price, aren't you?"

"No, sir. I don't think so. At least, not really."

"Evil," Staymore repeated, ignoring him. "How are your dear parents?" he went on with a sudden smile.

Oh golly, Evelyn thought, this is it! "Very well, sir, thank you. I had a letter from Mum last week. Uh—why do you ask, sir?"

"Good." The smile vanished. A pause. "Are you happy at this school?"

"Yes, sir!" Evelyn lied enthusiastically in his confusion. What was Staymore hinting at? He couldn't see any pattern in the questions. Could he be going to throw him out of the school? He couldn't do that! Oh yes he could, Evelyn reflected. But then maybe he was just trying to be friendly. Grasping at this sudden hope, Evelyn went on:

"I'm sure it's true what they say, sir, about your school-days being the happiest days of your life!" Evelyn attempted a smile with the words, but it faded as he saw Staymore's scowl.

"Rubbish!" the headmaster hissed, "you don't come to school to be happy, you little wretch. You come here to learn—to love Almighty God. To prepare yourself for the only reason God put you on this earth. To *die!*"

"Yes, sir," Evelyn mumbled, shaking with fear.

Staymore looked at the little boy. And hated him. There wasn't an ounce of goodness in the child. It sometimes taxed his faith to have to believe that arrogant, snivelling wretches such as this were made in the image of God.

"You're an evil little boy, Price."

No reply.

"Aren't you?" Staymore demanded.

Evelyn looked down at the floor. "No, sir," he said quietly.

Staymore could feel the blood come to his face and a pulse in his temple pounding. My God, this brat must be taught! He pushed back his chair, rose, strode to his canes, selected one that was long and thick. He took it from the stand. It looked like a twig in the meat of his hand. He flexed it in the air. It made a satisfying swish. He turned and faced the child.

"I'm going to thrash you, Price."

The boy shuffled. He looked at his headmaster; with quivering lips asked: "What for?"

Staymore was infuriated. The impertinence! How dare the child question his headmaster! Quickly he strode to him and grasping him by an ear propelled him towards a large leather arm-chair.

"Get over that! Take off your trousers!" he snarled.

Evelyn's moment of resistance was gone. He leant over the chair, pulled down his trousers, let them below his knees. He bent over, holding with his outstretched arms to the arms of the chair.

"The pants! The pants!" Staymore snarled.

Evelyn took down his underpants.

"Hah!" Staymore exulted. And standing over the boy, he lifted the cane till it touched the roof of the room. He paused. The boy's bottom was round and smooth—deliciously pink. For a moment Staymore stood and stared at it. Dear Lord, I do this for you, he thought.

Then he brought down his arm.

Even though he was tensed and waiting for it, the first cut of the cane came so hard that it knocked the breath from Evelyn's body and he couldn't help gasping. He'd never been so badly hurt before. Thrash! Down came the second stroke. God the pain. Another. How many more could there be? One was usually told. This wasn't fair. He wanted to cry. The fourth blow. He wouldn't cry. Wouldn't.

The Reverend Sullivan Staymore hit the fourteen-year-old

boy eight times. With all his strength and weight. But so great was his skill that each blow struck precisely the same place and when, panting a little, he finally ended, there was only one red weal on the boy's quivering backside.

"That will do for the moment," Staymore said, relaxing.

With clumsy hands, Price began to scoop up his underpants and trousers. As he did so, Staymore noticed the boy was crying. Excellent. He had started to break.

Trousers on, Price turned to his headmaster. He had managed to stop his tears and with the back of a hand now brushed their stains from his cheeks. It was the custom at this school to shake hands after a flogging and he held out a hand. Staymore took the offered hand and gripped it. After a second, Price tried to draw it back, but Staymore held it hard in his grasp.

"Now, my dear, sit down. Make yourself comfortable. Let us have a little chat." He let go Evelyn's hand.

The boy stood for a moment—wanting to turn and flee from the unbearable pain in his behind. Reluctantly, he moved to the leather chair over which he had just been thrashed. Staymore went to his desk, lay his cane along it and settled himself comfortably in his swivel-chair. He reached in a drawer and took out a box of chocolates. As he tore off their cellophane wrapper, he saw that Price was still standing.

"Sit down, child!"

"If you don't mind, sir, I'd rather stand," Evelyn replied respectfully.

"*Sit,*" Staymore ordered, staring expressionlessly into the youth's eyes.

Holding to the arms of the chair like a cripple, Evelyn slowly lowered himself, trembling, into it. He winced with pain as his bottom met the leather and altered position to favour his unflogged side. But it didn't seem to help much, for he started to cry again at the pain and the unfairness of it.

"That's better." Staymore smiled. He scooped a chocolate from the box and, his eyes never leaving Evelyn, slopped it into his mouth.

"Would you care for one of these?"

But Price only shook his head and started to cry even more. "Can I go now, please, sir?" he pleaded through tears.

"Brace up!" Staymore suddenly ordered sharply. "What sort of despicable little wretch are you—whining like a girl? Get a grip on yourself."

Price tried to. Not very successfully. "I'm sorry, sir," he said weakly.

"Humph!" Staymore slurped over another chocolate. Then he altered his expression into one which he imagined expressed comradeship. "My dear, I want you to tell me your problems. Feel quite free to confide in me. Tell me what's worrying you."

Price stopped crying. Said nothing.

"You can feel quite at ease. For though I am your headmaster, remember I am also a priest—and anything you wish to tell me comes under the inviolable secrecy of the Confessional."

Price's voice trembled a little as he blinked up at the headmaster. "Why was I beaten?" he asked.

Staymore looked at him in a forgiving way. "Because you're an evil little boy, Price." He paused and his eyes once more were slits. "Aren't you?"

Price was broken. "Yes, sir," he admitted humbly, "if you say so."

"I don't say so, boy. You do. I want you to confess your evil to me now—to freely try and rid your soul of all the wicked things you've done."

Evelyn Price thought quickly and as hard as he could. It wasn't easy because he was still paining badly. Staymore's already beaten me, he reasoned, he won't punish me more. There isn't any harm in owning up. It might even get me out of here quicker. I'm quite safe. He's even mentioned the secrecy of the Confessional. There might be something in getting flogged before he's found out the crime after all. Otherwise, he might have beat me even worse.

So he reasoned in his innocence.

"Well, sir, I—I walked out of a masters-only door yesterday."

"I know. I know," Staymore lied petulantly. "You also had

20

your hands in your pockets last night. But these are only break-ing school rules, boy. They are not really *sins*."

"Oh. No. I suppose not." Evelyn had never looked at it that way before.

"Well?" the headmaster's voice cut in on his thoughts.

"Yes—well—uh . . . there isn't anything else I can think of."

"Don't lie to me, Price." Staymore glowered.

"I'm not, sir, honestly."

"What about your drinking, eh?"

"I've never drunk anything, sir!"

"No? No? And you've never taken drugs either, I suppose?"

"No, sir!" Price was frightened. Very.

"And now I suppose you're going to tell me that you've never even smoked a cigarette?"

"No, sir. Only once. Last year at home. At Christmas. I—I felt sick."

"*Liar!*" Staymore screamed. He snatched open a drawer of his desk, flung out a crumpled pack of cigarettes. "Whose are these, then? Whose are these, eh?"

Price was near hysteria. The tears pumped from his eyes. This was an expellable offence. He leaned forward imploringly in his chair. "I swear to you, sir. I never smoke. I don't, I don't know anything about those cigarettes. They're not mine. No, I swear by Almighty God!"

"There's no need to take the Name of the Lord in vain, Evelyn," Staymore smoothly replied. "I know you don't smoke."

Evelyn flumped back in his chair, started to giggle hysteri-cally.

"I also know what it is that you *do* do." Staymore went on, picking up his cane from the desk. "I know. I know what horrible thoughts of avarice are in your heart." He slowly stood, began to swish the cane in the air. "And all alone, when you think no one can see you, *I* know what your hands—the hands that will rot—are doing with the things that do not belong to them!" He issued his final words in a hiss of disgust.

Their effect was strange.

Evelyn rolled and twitched in the big leather arm-chair in

laughter that grew more and more frenzied—till suddenly he was perfectly still. His eyes gaped. His lips flecked and frothed. His tongue jerked out of place in his mouth. His body went stiff in the chair.

Staymore looked at him—and was filled with such peace as must reward the saints. This was a veritable exorcism. The slime of Satan oozed even now from the wretch's lips. Staymore went and knelt once more by the crucifix. Thank you, dear Lord, he prayed, for yet another conquest over the Devil's minions.

Then he rose, went to a phone on his desk; dialled the school infirmary. "This is the headmaster. Send the doctor to my study. There's a boy here who seems to be having a fit."

He replaced the phone and looked once more with satisfaction at the rigid boy in his chair. He was sad he couldn't stay to hear the doctor's verdict. But alas it was the twenty-third of September and he was obliged to go to London.

For tomorrow at ten-thirty the Reverend Sullivan Staymore had a train to catch.

CHAPTER 2

THE railroad had run through her life.

It had clothed her, fed her. It had housed her close to its tracks and all through her childhood its engines had shaken the windows of her nights and steamed and sucked and rumbled through her dreams. Now, at thirty-two, she had come back to it. As Ann Cross stood on the London platform looking out along down the tracks, admiring their strength and unbending straightness, they seemed an unbroken cord joining her here-and-now to the past.

Ann's father had earned their living at a station. As a porter. But not at a vast metropolitan sprawl like this. His was a sideline country outpost in the North—so little used that when the railway began to lose money it was one of the first stations to be ruled uneconomic and closed. At such a place, in such a job, her father had little work and even less responsibility. But the lines worn deep in his forehead, the nervous tic that fluttered his right eye suggested that he carried not luggage but the worries of the world on his back.

He was compulsively anxious.

Almost anything, real or imaginary, could fill him with dread. As minute a question as whether to wear black or brown socks could bring on agonies of nail-gnawing indecision. And there were days when his deep foreboding at the prospect of cycling the short distance from his house to the station where he worked became such that he was unable to rise from his bed.

He was not like his daughter Ann. She had been born with a mind that was cold and clear and did not see shadows—and which, for as long back as she could remember, had despised her father.

And mother also. For the woman was his perfect soul-mate: jittering, neurotic, spasmodic—terrified. With an inability to manage which turned their tiny house into even more of a slum than their multitude of children and a minuscule income called for. All she seemed able to do was breed. By the time Ann was fourteen, she had seven younger brothers and sisters. Looking back over the years now, she remembered her mother as almost always pregnant, certainly always unable to cope; her father growing more confused and cowering with each new child; their house too cramped to contain them all and so frail and close to the railway line that it shook so it seemed it would come to pieces with each passing train.

Ann realised her parents must have gone irrevocably to pieces long before. More and more she grew to despise their weakness, the endless quivering that was their lives. In reaction to it she began to worship strength. In any form. She watched herself unpityingly and any weakness, whatever of her parents, she found within her she destroyed. She locked an iron grip around her mind and heart. And she grew strong. Strong enough to record one day with emotionless logic that her mother was insane; to report that fact to the men who eventually came and took the woman to the hospital. Strong enough to see her father

24

would follow her mother into insanity and that staying with him could only endanger her own persona.

So the railway lines that were her nights one night took her away.

She was fifteen.

Any sorrow she might have felt at leaving her younger brothers and sisters she dispelled. If they were tough, they'd survive. If not, they didn't deserve to. It wasn't nice, but it was life. As she was tough herself she appreciated that it had to be so.

Her train had snaked into London in the cold of an autumn morning. Never before had she been to a major city and, watching with her face pressed close to the window as they unendingly slowed through the sameness of suburbia finally to the station, she was seized by a sense of the world's great hugeness —and how small she was herself. All the fear that she so despised in her parents came bubbling up in her. Almost all her money had gone on the fare—what would she do now? Where would she go? The city was an incredible mouth that would swallow and destroy her. The fears accumulated till they grew to a screaming in her mind—and long after the train had stopped and emptied in the station Ann Cross sat motionless on her seat in the compartment. The fear came near to overwhelming her. Had it, she might have joined her mother in the asylum. But a part of her mind fought back at it. And won. Then a cold bitter peace came into her and she got up and went out onto the station and from that moment she was mistress of her mind and did not feel fear again.

Her plans were vague. She intended finding a job. Quite what it'd be or how she'd find it, she wasn't sure. But she bought a ticket on the Underground to central London, which was where she guessed whatever it was she was looking for was most likely to be.

The year was 1955. But even then as Ann Cross, fifteen-year-old girl from the North came out of the Underground to the daylight of central London, the scene before her seemed a crazy turmoil. For a second she shrank back on the sidewalk, dazzled by the people, traffic, noise, onrush of it all. For a second her mind superimposed on the scene a picture of the little country town near her home. Then the picture faded and she smiled at the bustling activity around her and knew she would never go home again.

She wasn't sure for how long, but Ann had just walked: gaping at the tall buildings, the multitudinous surge of every possible kind of person. This was more than a city. It was a world. And it was all before her! She gave a mental whoop of excitement at the vitality of it all. All these people, action—opportunity!

Then she realised she was hungry.

Looking for somewhere to eat, she had seen a sign for a cafe down a side-road and had gone to it and stared in through a window crammed with continental food. It was lunch-time and the place was doing good business. Office workers filed in a line past a counter where they collected and paid for food, then took it to tables to eat. Ann noticed prices in the window. They were low. She went in and joined the line.

Reaching the counter she ordered coffee and two chocolate cakes from a jovial little man behind it and took them to a back table where she sat and toyed with them and took in the scene around her.

The place had a brisk turn-over. No one lingered over their food and when they'd finished they got up and left. Ann was impressed with the people. The men wore snappy suits. The girls, some of them little older than herself, glittered with makeup and strutted on skyscraper heels. They seemed urbane, assured. She studied them, panning out her cakes, till all at once the restaurant began to empty and a hard-faced bright-blond waitress started clearing up. Soon only the waitress, herself, and the fat little man behind the counter were left—and Ann realised that an interlude was over and it was time to move on and face up to life. She turned her attention to the remains of her final cake.

"Finished then, have you?"

She looked up. The waitress stood over her, gave a brief superior smile and before Ann could even answer, picked up her plate and stacked other plates on top of it—squashing her cake. Arms filled with plates then, she turned from the table. Ann was so angry she didn't even think. Of its own accord her leg darted out from under the table in front of the waitress's feet.

The result was ecstatic.

The girl tripped. Her legs shot up. The plates crashed down. She plummeted into an adjoining table, sending it and everything on it smashing to the floor beneath her. The little man jerked round from his counter. The waitress was large and her impact like a hand-grenade. He stared at the mess, speechless. His face changed colour. Veins bulged in his forehead.

At last he burst out: "You vool! Again you break plates. You vill to ruin me—ya? *Ghet out!* I vire you!"

The waitress picked herself up; forgetting what tripped her, faced her employer with equal anger. And a fuller vocabulary.

"Don't you bloody shout at me!" she shouted, "You—you—kraut. And you can stuff your lousy job—see? I'm *leaving!*"

She tore off her apron, threw it to the floor, kicked viciously at the broken crockery round her feet and stomped towards the door, deliberately upsetting another table on the way.

"Ghet out!" he screamed after her.

But she had already gone.

The experience lasted hardly a minute. But it left Ann trembling with laughter she could hardly suppress. The man was glaring after his departed waitress now, frothing with half-voiced curses. So this little guy was the boss! She had an inspiration. As he turned round to look at her, she got up from her table and demurely bent down and began to gather the broken scattered plates from the floor.

"Nein! You mustn't!" he called out to her.

But she ignored him and went on till her arms were full of plates. Then she rose, smiled at him and carried them to the counter.

"Ach! Dank you—you are wery kint." He took the pieces from her. She went back for more.

"Vait! I vill help!" he called and scurried from behind the

counter, knelt down beside her and started to gather fragments of crockery.

"Zat girl—vat a pitch!" he wheezed. "Like von of za vamily I treat her so gut. Unt zen—ach!" he shrugged disgustedly.

"She did seem kind of . . . clumsy," Ann replied sympathetically.

The man snorted back in outrage—and went on to detail all the sins of the waitress and his own incredible goodness to her. But Ann wasn't listening. A single thought filled her mind: she needed work; he needed a waitress. It wasn't glamorous, but it was a job.

As they carried the last fragments to the counter, she ventured, "You'll need someone else now, won't you?"

"Ya." He nodded unhappily, putting the broken plates in a trash can.

Seeing that he wasn't taking the hint, she went on bluntly: "How about me?"

He turned to face her. His eyes narrowed. She saw a sort of gleam behind them that she didn't understand. He looked her up and down rather disparagingly for some time. "You?" he asked as if the idea was incredible.

"Yes," she replied, returning his stare.

He raised his eyebrows, turned down the corners of his mouth and shrugged. "How olt you are, huh?"

"Eighteen," Ann lied. It was a brave lie. And a transparent one. Her wide-spaced cool green eyes were older than her age all right, but her body was straight and clearly pre-pubescent.

"Hah! You're eighteen, I'm ninety-vif, ya?" he chortled.

Ann didn't share the joke. Abruptly he snapped off his laughter and told her stonily: "I gif you vif pound a veek. Foot unt bet. No more. Nozink. You break plates, I take from pay."

And that had been it.

Her first job. The start of it all. On her feet and working twelve hours a day. Non-stop. Washing dishes and cleaning and clearing and running to every strident order of the fat little cafe owner who smiled a lot—but only to his customers.

28

What a long way that was from here—and in more than just distance—Ann thought, looking down the platform to where her train was now pulling in. Still . . . she was grateful for that little cafe. It had given her a better education in life than she could have had at any school.

She had lived and worked there for two years.

And in that time she learnt all right. From watching. From listening. To the fights between the cafe owner and his wife, the conversations of the hundreds of different people who came to the cafe. And she changed. From hick girl to hard woman. She grew. Up and out. And the embryonic ideas she left home with grew as firm as her figure. She saw that life in all its complexity could be distilled to just a single thing—having.

Ann Cross knew that she had to have.

And because she was strong that she would.

The typists who bustled in for lunch had. Not much, but much more than her. Above them, secretaries had more still. As she worked, Ann studied them, learnt of their worlds. And she learnt of the worlds beyond them. By reading. Avidly. In every second of her little spare time. Not from any joy in books, but in deliberate quest of knowledge and to improve herself. And what she read increased her understanding—and ambition. She came to see that for her there were two ways of having: marry money, or make it. The first was out of the question. She couldn't weaken herself by submitting to a man. As for the second, she'd never have the chance to achieve it at the cafe, so she determined to move to an orbit of greater opportunities.

But there were no stars in the cool green eyes of Ann Cross. She was young, red-haired, fresh-skinned, with an attractive figure. Yet she never for a moment considered the dream of so many young girls—to model or act. Instead, she saved her money. And twice a week at night she went to secretarial college.

It was the roughest period of her life. The work in the cafe was crippling. Night school wasn't cheap and to save money on the bus fare she used to walk all the way there and when she arrived was sometimes so tired that it was all she could do to stay awake.

But she was tough with herself. And grew tougher.

By the time she was seventeen, she had qualified as a short-hand typist. As soon as she had, she quit the cafe and got another job.

It was copy typist in an Advertising Agency. It was hard work and not that better paid than her previous job, but she was delighted with it. She was in business! And anyway, she didn't stay at the bottom long. Six months in all. Six months in a typing-pool with brainless, boy-mad little typists. Six months as the lowest form of life in the place apart from the half-mad old bag who pushed round the coffee-wagon. It was quite long enough to absorb the basics of the business. To see that advertising was an area where those who were tough and hustled hard could get on. It couldn't have suited her more.

The next rung above her in the ladder was secretary—attached if possible to just one man; and the better paid the man, the better paid the secretary. It was a job for which Ann was qualified. But, as she soon found, there was intensive competition for secretarial posts and prospective employers weren't keen to hire a girl who hadn't already held the position in at least one agency. So Ann decided to promote herself. She forged a glowing letter of reference about her, presented it and herself at another agency—and got a job. At almost double her previous pay. As a secretary and to an executive.

Boasting the almost unbelievably British name of Jonathan Ewing-Gore, Ann's new boss was well educated, well dressed—and doing well. And, she soon saw, was going to do better. She'd fallen lucky. This was a man with whom she could rise.

She became the perfect secretary. By working hard. By getting to know her boss—so well she could almost read his mind; could sense his wishes and execute them almost before he knew them himself. In short, she made herself indispensable. And by the end of her first year in advertising, she was secure. Secured to a leading Account Man. It was a level at which many less ambitious women might have settled happily—and then maybe begun to look quietly round for a man they could wed.

The thought made her smile.

That had hardly even been the beginning. Perhaps even this wasn't, she reflected—and her mind came back to the present and she became aware of what was happening around her.

The platform had filled, the train come to rest. People were milling about it. She watched them: getting on, getting off, waiting by the train—all so pointlessly. They didn't know it but all their bustle was a sham. They would never go anywhere. They were travel-weary and beaten even before they started their journeys. Weak ordinary little people. The fact that Ann had risen from among them made her despise them the more.

She turned and signalled a porter to put her bags on the train. Then she followed him on. When he had safely established her luggage in her first-class compartment, she sat down and looked out the window. She'd got here much too early. It wasn't a thing she usually did. But then today, of all days, for some reason she felt that she had time—all the time in the world. Certainly enough now to go out and buy a magazine.

Ann got up and got off the train. She moved back into the heart of the station and, as she did, her mind began to go back again and she let it.

Jonathan Ewing-Gore.

He was nobody's fool. He had seen that Ann was more than just good secretarial material and had the sense to realise that the more senior the place he gave her on his team, the more she could do for him. So he promoted her. Made her his assistant— Assistant Account Executive. It wasn't a much better paid position, but the difference between it and secretary was like the gulf between labour and management. Even now, the title sounded rich in her brain.

The new job wasn't without its problems. There'd been a lot to learn. But Jonathan was behind her and knew what she needed to and she picked his brains. Till she learned most everything that he had. About how an Agency ran and what made it pay. About buying space and time, producing an ad

31

in print or on film, marketing, merchandising, what was a good advertisement and what wasn't. Most important, she learnt the techniques of selling and conning and cajoling—and all vital—keeping the sacred clients from whom all business sprang.

This was the executive's primary job. If he did it well, in the end he might get to jingle accounts in his pocket like so much small change. If he didn't, he'd get fired.

Ann did it well.

She devoted all of her faculties, all of her time to studying her clients, learning their likes and dislikes and, where possible, their weaknesses—and how to exploit them. If she guessed, for instance, that a client had a liking for the ladies, she would scout round till she found girls she could pay to oblige him. And she would provide them free and in ever-ready stream—so long as the client never got troublesome. If he did, she'd just cease to supply. Of course nothing was ever overtly mentioned. But her message got understood just the same.

Pandering and plotting and pimping like this Ann got on well with her clients and never lost an account. And so the years went their gentle way to wherever years go.

Till one morning when she was twenty-two she realised she was in a rut.

She'd had raises in pay and was now earning well and well thought of, but she was no longer satisfied. Her official status was still Assistant Account Executive. She'd grown to abhore that word "assistant." It was time to move up.

Which meant it was time for Jonathan to go.

She was sorry about that. He'd taught her most of what she knew and helped her get where she was and for a time she had admired him. For he was slick and competent and seemed strong. But one day, under more than usual stress, he had gone out and got drunk at lunch-time and been incapable of working that afternoon. He had only done it once. But it was a weakness. She despised that. And in her mind it came to justify and lay the seeds for what she would later do.

It was very simple. When no one else was in the office, she typed two letters. Then she hid them in her desk. And waited.

She waited some time—months—before the moment she wanted came, the moment when business pressures on Jonathan were at absolute maximum.

Then she went to his boss.

A company director called Ackroyd, he was a thin, middle-aged man who had tried, but failed, to mask the signs of his humble origins. Ann had noted that he disliked and felt threatened by Jonathan. Equally, she knew he respected her for her efficient grasp of her job. Now she faced him with every show of embarrassment.

"I don't know how to say this, Mr. Ackroyd."

"Yes, Ann?"

"I'm not even sure I should."

"Go on."

"It's not that I don't feel loyal towards Jonathan. I do. It's just that my loyalty to the firm comes first."

"Quite right. So it should!"

Ann then proceeded to tell him what she felt he was hoping to hear: that Jonathan was failing; was often incapably drunk. That for months she'd been doing all his work for him.

Ackroyd put on a show of grave concern, but beneath it, Ann could see, was delighted. He thanked her for her commendable loyalty and promised to look into the matter.

Then Ann went back to her office and took out the two letters she had previously written. One was to an important client. A masterpiece of abuse. She signed Jonathan's name to it with a skill which would have made a professional forger proud. Then she read through and sealed the other letter. This was anonymous. To Jonathan's wife. Informing the woman that her husband was having an affair with his secretary. It was a lie, but Ann knew it would achieve what she wanted just the same.

She sealed and mailed both letters.

The next day, Jonathan came late to the office. As soon as she saw him, Ann could tell he was harassed to breaking-point. The letter to his wife had arrived.

"You look like you could use a stiff drink," she told him.

He stared at her without replying. There was clearly nothing in life he wanted so much.

"Go on! Why don't you? I'll take care of everything here."

He looked at her searchingly a moment, then nodded. "Yeah. I think I might have a quick one. All hell's broken loose at home."

Ann nodded sympathetically.

"You'll be a love and hold the fort?"

"Don't worry. I'll take care of everything!"

And she did. Took the telephone call from the irate client to whom she'd sent the abusive letter. And when the man demanded to speak to Jonathan, took care of everything by explaining she had orders that her boss wasn't to be bothered and that anyhow he never got back from the pubs till three. But would the client like to speak to Mr. Ackroyd, Jonathan's superior, she wondered.

He would. And did. In no uncertain way.

With the result that when Jonathan finally and unsteadily returned, he was summoned into Ackroyd's office. And fired.

He had been too drunk to defend himself or understand what he was supposed to have done and had come to Ann for help and explanation. But she hadn't been there. For just after he came out of Ackroyd's office, she went in. To get briefed on her new job.

His.

And so she moved up another rung.

The new job was less demanding than she expected. The work was much the same as she'd been doing before, and, although she now had the responsibility for initiating it, she also had an assistant of her own to help carry it out. If the job was no more demanding though, it was much more rewarding, for her salary was raised to correspond with her higher status and she was even given a modest expense account.

It was the beginning of prosperity.

She lived in a small and inexpensive apartment. She didn't drink, didn't smoke, didn't drive. She watched her food and dressed cleverly. She was able to live off her expense account

34

and almost everything she earned she saved. With her savings she bought shares. They appreciated. At that time there was no capital gains tax.

Five years after taking Jonathan's job, Ann Cross was worth twenty-five thousand pounds.

As for her private life? She didn't have any. She knew or consorted with no one not in some way connected with business: clients, suppliers, prospective clients, senior members of the firm. Her job was all her life.

After a while, though, she found that her life wasn't all she wanted it to be.

As time went on she grew increasingly dissatisfied. Perhaps because the appetite for having grows the more you have—and the essence of reaching for the sky is that you never touch it.

Perhaps because, though Ann was tough, able, in a senior position, she was also stuck.

She could go no further because, competent though she was, she'd been born with a handicap. She was a woman. And the business world, and maybe all the world, was run by men. They'd let her get so far, but no farther. Though she was now more able than Ackroyd, though she could fabricate ways to discredit him, she realised that—even if she got him fired—she'd never get his job. Invisible barriers were barriers none the less and there was no way to break through them to her next objective—the board.

It had called for a period of serious reassessment, she reflected, looking over the magazines and paperbacks on the station bookstand. She bought a financial paper, an advertising periodical, a fashion magazine. Yes. And when she had thought it all out, it boiled down to a single possibility.

The only way to get right to the top was to leave that agency and start one of her own.

But although that was easy to say, it wasn't to do. The situation was one of those vicious circles. To start a company you need money. The bank will lend you money—if you have a business. But how do you get it if you're not *in* business, not already a company?

35

Ann realised the only way would be to take accounts from her existing firm; but she was a realist and could see no reason why clients should move their advertising from an established competent agency to a brand-new, untried concern—even if they knew its founder. No. There would have to be some way of persuading them.

Or making them.

It was at this point that she thought of blackmail.

It was a good idea. It worked. Nearly everyone has something in his life he doesn't want known. Get hold of that and you have a hold on the man. To a point. And Ann's point wasn't that far. After all, she wasn't asking them to part with their own money—just their company's advertising allocation. And she wasn't going to lose them out on that, either. For, after all, wasn't she good at her job? And wasn't she going to cram her new company with all the best talent in town? It was a persuasive argument. Especially when backed with letters and photos and facts.

They hadn't all been easy to come by. She was able to photograph two of her married clients on the job with girls she provided herself. But to try to compromise or incriminate the rest, she had to hire private detectives—the most unscrupulous she could find. She had phones tapped, letters intercepted; where necessary, houses entered and documents removed. It didn't always work. Some of her clients escaped her investigations. And she spent a considerable sum of her savings in finding out what she did. But in the end it was worth it and she had enough. Gently but inexorably she tightened her grip on a good chunk of business and she became so adept at sniffing out unsavoury facts and playing on a latent sense of guilt that in one case she even insinuated her way into securing a man's account without ever learning what it was he was afraid that she knew and would tell.

Business securely in hand, she had gone to the bank. They had floated her. She gathered a team of bright men around her and worked them hard. At the end of her first fiscal year her agency was paying its way and was doing as well or better for its initially reluctant clients than their previous agents. And now that they had legitimate reasons for being with her, they felt happier and Ann let her grip on them seem to soften and saw that they were pimped and pleased and pandered to as always before.

Of course it hadn't all gone smoothly. She had lost one block of business almost as soon as she got it. The man she'd been blackmailing was basically moral and didn't want to give her work and she had to squeeze him hard. Finally, because he loved his wife and children desperately and could never bear them to know what Ann knew, he gave her his account. But he had been deeply disturbed about it. How deeply Ann found out only one week after she landed his business.

The man was dead.

And it was rather suitable that she should be thinking of him here at a railway station. He'd committed suicide by throwing himself under a train.

It was too bad. But the man was weak and had come up against her and she was strong and had destroyed him. It was the law of existence: the meek and mild would always bow to might—and he was just a speck of sand in the universe of that fact. Ann was sorry. But chiefly at losing his business.

She had kept her other clients. Alive. And with her. And two years after forming her company she met her main chance.

It comes in most everyone's life—the tide that can sweep you to fortune. Ann's was called Frank. He was soft-spoken, in his mid-forties and the hardest man she'd met. His background was as small-time as Ann's but his success much bigger. From nowhere he had worked his way to managing directorship of a consumer durables company whose advertising expenditure alone amounted to nearly one million pounds a year. Ann knew that his account alone could so alter the profitability of her company that, could she land it, she'd become a rich woman overnight.

She set her hounds to sniff out the skeleton in Frank's life, to find that one shameful incident we all must have. Only he hadn't. He was a textbook straight guy. Perhaps because like Ann he'd been so involved in his work he had time for nothing else—and unlike her had been honest. She didn't worry about the reasons why, though—simply about the fact that here was the most vital man in her life and she had nothing on him. There must be another way. She thought. And remembered her very first assessment of the ways to having: make money or marry it.

Marriage.

The prospect made her whole being go cold. She would have to submit herself to another human being—a thing she had never done. She would have to love, honour, obey. Grow up! She suddenly told herself. She need only make a pretence of these things. In very little time her strength would win through and her husband would be obeying her. No. Her real problem was how to get him to marry her. All her life she had avoided intimate contact with men, had never seen any need to go beyond an occasional flirtation with a client—and never let that reach its conclusion. Now, inexperienced as she was in the ways of wooing, she would have to somehow win over this tough intelligent businessman. It would hardly be easy.

It wasn't.

She worked harder at making Frank love her than anything she'd ever done. And in the end she failed.

But she succeeded in marrying him. There she was lucky. For, like her, he was surprisingly naïve in affairs of the heart; their comparable backgrounds gave them much in common; and she was an attractive woman.

One year after meeting Frank she managed to get herself pregnant by him. And then he did the gentlemanly thing.

Before their marriage she made a show of selling her agency so she could devote herself full-time to being a wife. In fact she simply passed it over to the ostensible control of a nominee. Then they married and she settled down into a hated charade of loving spouse and, later, the terrible actuality of motherhood. But all the time she worked on her husband. Subtly. Delicately. Constantly. First insinuating that his firm's advertising should be moved; then reinforcing her point, wherever possible, by sabotaging the efforts of their existing agency; finally by finding out and feeding back company information to her own firm—so that when they eventually came to pitch for the business they would know exactly what was wanted. And supply it. The process took time. She had to be careful that her husband never realised what she was doing or that she was still connected with the agency. But in the end she won through. She was too well placed to lose.

Then a child was born to them. And it paid dividends—by giving her a hold on her husband. For now even this tough shrewd businessman had a weakness. And would become soft and manageable—when he saw his son.

Ann's agency made money.

From a distance she manipulated the reins of power and her husband never knew. She was so pleased with the situation that she decided to consolidate her grip on him even further by producing another child. And she did.

One year after the birth of her second son, she saw the writing on the wall.

For some time, feeling secure in her hold over her husband's advertising revenue, she had been cutting down on staff—maximising profits at the expense of providing a proper service. Suddenly the company sensed it and weren't happy. Ann exerted all her indirect influence, but it wasn't enough. Long before anyone without such close family ties could have, she realised there was nothing she could do to prevent her agency's losing the account.

Swiftly, discreetly she placed her firm on the market. She was a shrewd negotiator. She had a highly prosperous enterprise to sell. No one guessed that within months its backbone would be torn out and it would be virtually valueless.

And so she sold her company. Together with all she had milked from it, that made her a wealthy woman. Worth in her own right a quarter of a million pounds.

Once the agency had gone, her reasons for staying with Frank had too. He was prosperous. But she was more so. And in business he could do nothing more for her.

She asked for a divorce.

Strangely, he didn't seem upset—or even surprised. That annoyed her. She had been through purgatories of pretence these last years and thought she had acted her part out well. Her annoyance vanished, though, when he agreed to the divorce and a respectable alimony as well—provided she conceded all custody of the children. Which she was only too glad to do.

And so Frank and Ann parted. With Ann in the eyes of the world the injured party. A woman repeatedly wronged who could endure it no more. That was the way she wanted it. That was what she got. They had too many influential acquaintances in common for her to wish the truth to be known.

Immediately after the divorce, she decided to get away. For the first time in her life she was tired. Drained. Her strength needed replenishing. All these years and she had never had a holiday—she would take one now. She had as much money to relax and do nothing with for as long as she wished. Not that she would do nothing. That would be weak. She'd plan her next business venture. But in a suitably opulent setting for a change, enjoying for almost the first time some of the fruits of her labours. In Paris. Yes. And as she wasn't in any hurry and it seemed a civilised way of getting there, she booked on the Golden Arrow. First class, of course.

And that, Ann Cross, she thought, is your life: from a third-class runaway ride to a first-class trip to the finest hotel in Paris. And here you are at Victoria Station, Friday the twenty-fourth of September, walking to your train.

Ann Cross.

A woman of thirty-two. Good-looking. Rich. Successful and strong. By some standards not an evil woman perhaps. Yet a woman who throughout her life stepped on those feebler than her; who drove a man to suicide; who for no other reason than that it suited her abandoned her husband and children.

Ann carried these things in her mind as she went to her platform and she recognised their truth—but could live with it. For what mattered above all was victory.

And she'd won.

But then, just as she climbed to her compartment, she had an unusual thought. If there's such a thing as justice, she thought—and smiled because she doubted there was—it would see me in hell.

CHAPTER 3

BILL Armstrong looked out into the mist and felt alone. And he was afraid.

And excited.

All of his life—his pleasures and failures—all that his twenty-five years had been and had done to form the man he was and now could not help but be, everything led to here. Here in the night. To this wooded country road outside the long drive of the house. Sitting in a stolen Ford in the moonless autumn watching a ground mist rise in swirling shapes that danced across the deserted road. Here with the only sound the throb of his veins in his ears. So like the beating of a heart.

So like the beating of the heart he had come to still.

He sat and thought. Everyone has to die. I'm going to die myself. The thing is while it lasts to live the best you can. This man has. I haven't. I've been born to it, bred and taught to it—but not been given it. My birthright. The really good life I deserve but haven't had.

So I'm the only child of a fine old family—great! And, sure enough, I start with every advantage. Prosperous parents, an expensive school. And I do all right there too. So I'm not the world's best at exams, perhaps, and fail to make the university—so what? The year I captain the football team we never get beaten once. And I don't just win every time I go into the ring, no one even takes me the distance!

Sure, it was good that time.

But then it was over. And after, there was all that jazz about getting a job. Job—puh! The only thing I'd been taught was how to be a gentleman, how to enjoy myself—and you didn't get paid for that. But the parents take it all so seriously, me never staying at the dreary jobs. Then that trouble over the girl. What was her name? Funny how you forget. And right on top of it—whammo! The knock-out. Suddenly right out of the blue the old man refusing to honour the poker debts anymore. And, as if that wasn't enough, soon after going and dropping dead and not a mention at all in the will. All to Mother. All to the gigolo the tramp went and married when the old man was barely cold . . .

Bill shuddered and cut off the memory. Life was rough enough without dredging up things that hurt from the past to make it worse. Think of the present, boy, of the good things, of why you're here. Think of your motor and your bird! Of the old Aston Martin and the young Australian. The motor goes like a bullet—so long as you pump in a gallon every eight miles or so. And the bird isn't slow either—so long as you pump out the sort of life she feels a gentleman ought to provide. But both, of course, cost.

So you're here.

Fate's funny. Everything's sort of inevitable. No job, no money, debts, the bird about to split—so naturally it calls for a drink. And there he is in the bar. Bertie, the rich little twerp who hero-worshipped me at school and I haven't seen since.

And we're shaking hands like brothers and he's buying and already had a few and two bars later on, he lays it on the line. The photo. The thin finger stabbing it. "Kill this man and I'll pay you five thousand pounds."

He isn't joking.

We go back to his place—God, what a palace—and the wad comes out. Three hundred "on account." What sort of fool would say no to that? And then I've got the photograph and the address. And I've sort of said yes and I'm in it. Committed. Good God, five thousand! There wasn't anything else I could do.

It wasn't the first time Bill Armstrong had been over the reasons for doing this thing in his mind. Each time he did it, he felt more justified, became more convinced. He was very convinced now as he reached forward and started the car.

Slowly he drove down the wooded country road in the dark from the drive of the house. What he needed was a place to leave the car. When you came to kill a man you didn't just motor right up to his door; you had to make your way silently, on foot—and that meant finding somewhere to hide the car. Somewhere it wouldn't be seen from the road. He'd stolen it, had taken care to leave no fingerprints, was sure it could not be traced back to him, but all the same wasn't going to take any chances.

After two hundred yards, he found a clear space by the edge of the woods. There was a track leading in through the trees. He pulled off the road onto it, drove a little way into the woods; turned the car round and parked it facing the way he had come. He put off the headlamps, took a flashlight, got out of the car and examined the marks his tyres had made. They were scant. The ground was hard and dry and beaten down over time by the passage of many wheels. This was a place where couples would come after the pubs had closed on warmer nights of the year.

He pulled back a glove and shone the flashlight at his watch. Nine-thirty. It seemed as good a time to do it as any other.

He carefully locked the doors of the car. Then began the walk out of the woods back towards the house.

When he reached the edge of the woods he turned off the flashlight and waited. After about five minutes his eyes grew accustomed to the night. And he went on. Quickly he walked down the narrow country road on the grass verge where his feet made little noise. The night was cold. His breath made wreaths of mist in the darkness. He drew up the collar of his tailor-made sports jacket round his neck—and was suddenly aware that he hadn't felt so sharp, so keenly alive, since the last time he went into the ring. It was good to be in action, in danger, again.

He swung up to the drive of the house. It was wide, tar-macked, with tall metal gates conveniently open. Bill stopped and peered up it. And at that moment his exhilaration died and he saw he was in trouble. He should have known every inch of that drive, the entire layout of the property, back-wards. He didn't. He should have learnt everything about the man and his habits precisely. He hadn't. All he had was an address, a name, a photograph. Too little to go forward blind into the mist upon and kill a strange man. But then . . . five thousand made up for a lot.

Bill began to walk up the drive.

It was lined with rhododendrons and he would have tried to crawl through them, but he didn't know how far he had to go and he figured that if he were caught it were better here in-nocently on the drive than skulking round in the bushes. So he decided to make his way straight up to the house.

And he did.

It was a long walk. Cold. With the mist making shapes like the law every yard of the way. But it stayed only mist and finally, shaky but undetected, Bill came to where the drive ended in a wide semi-circle of gravel round a large, square-fronted house.

He crouched back for cover into the bushes. And began to wonder how he could ever get to that house. Along the whole huge frontage there wasn't a curtain drawn and light blazed

45

out from what seemed scores of windows like the searchlights of a concentration camp. Worse, people sat round a dinner table in a room directly facing him. Worse still, the gravelled space from here to the house was at least fifty yards wide. If he made a break across it now, he was sure to be seen or heard. He could try to crawl over on his face, but gravel isn't for crawling on and besides, to anyone deciding to come out the front door he'd look as clearly up to no good as a bishop in a whorehouse.

There must be some other way. Like working round through the shrubbery to the back of the house? Not on your life! He'd make a murderous row. Might leave footprints. Would be sure to snag telltale bits of his jacket on every bush he came across.

No. There was only one chance. To wait till those people left the dining room. Then go on the way he started. Blatant, assured. To walk straight up to the house, hope the front door wasn't locked. And just go in.

Bill waited.

And five minutes after the people in the dining room got up from the table and left he came out of the bushes and began to saunter across the drive—looking as casually confident as if this were his own estate. But not feeling it. Inside his mind he was naked. Exposed at any moment to a challenge from the night, the bark of a dog. And each step of his feet on the gravel sounded like guns going off in his ears. It wasn't easy to go forward. He wanted too much to turn and run, but because he'd started he kept on. And, as chance would have it, for all the noise he made and all the time he took to reach it, he wasn't seen or heard by anyone inside the house at all.

He got to the front door and stopped there. It was a large door. Thick and heavy. The kind of door that said clearer than words: "Keep out." He looked at it—and was seized with desperation. There was too much behind him, far too much in front. What was he doing here anyhow? Even if he had the guts to go in there, how was he going to find the man? How would he deal with him when he had? It was all very well rubbing someone out in your mind, and just collecting five grand. But when you stood in the dark outside this door . . . hell!

46

Bill stood under the night. Too frightened to turn, too frightened to think much—and then all at once he was angry. Dammit, he'd given his word. He'd done a lot of things in his time but never broken that. What sort of chicken am I anyhow, he thought. If they catch me at this stage I can always say I'm lost and just need directing.

He pressed his ear to the door and listened.

If anything waited for him on the other side it made no noise. He looked at the doorknob. Ha! It was probably locked anyway. That'd settle everything. If it was, he'd just turn round and go home. Honour would be satisfied. He'd have done all he reasonably could.

He reached out his gloved hand and turned the knob. The door was not locked. In fact it was so perfectly oiled, balanced, and hinged, that, silently and with no help from Bill at all, it swung wide open before him.

He found himself staring into a hall.

It was empty. He stood and looked at it. The hall contained overcoats, boots, outdoor clothes, and a stand with walking sticks and guns. Directly in front of the door a passage stretched away into the house and from the end of it he could hear the sound of voices. Doors ran off the passageway and in the hall itself was a door to his left, a door to his right.

Bill stepped into the hall, closed the front door as quietly as he could behind him. He stood there a moment uncertain what to do, then his eyes fell on the stick and gun stand and he moved quietly across to it. He contemplated taking a gun for a moment but decided instead on a stick and took a heavy one from the stand. He felt the balance of it in his hand, struck an imaginary blow with it in the air and began to feel better. But he didn't feel that way for long. There was a voice getting louder from a room at the end of the passage. Someone was coming this way. Bill looked around him frantically. There was nowhere in the hall to hide. Just the door to his left, the one to his right. But which? Bill stood looking at them in an agony of indecision. The voice had stopped now, had translated itself to unseen footsteps coming down the passage towards him. God, which door? Perhaps because he was right-handed, Bill went through the door on his right.

Into a dead-end.

It was a toilet. The light was on and he could see that the only door was that through which he had come. And it was too late to go back. The footsteps were coming nearer and nearer. Heavily, steadily. The steps of a man.

Bill flattened himself behind the door. Maybe the man wouldn't come in here. He listened as the footsteps got closer, stopped just outside his door. He held his breath, pressed back against the wall, lifted the stick. For a moment nothing happened. Then the doorknob turned, the door opened, a man came in, started to shut the door—and saw him.

Bill clubbed the man with the stick and all his weight behind it as hard as he could on the head.

The blow smashed the man sideways; he pivoted round, cracked face-on into a wall—then his knees went and he slithered down the wall to the floor. He didn't move anymore. Bill looked down at him and started to tremble from all the tension of the past half hour that the blow had released. He was trembling so badly that he had to make a conscious effort to control the muscles of his arm as he shut the door and engaged the bolt.

Bill sagged back against a wall. After a moment he grew conscious that he was breathing in pants and the sweat was standing cold on his face. He felt hysterically relieved. He wanted to sing. He looked at his victim. The man was small and portly and balding. That'll teach you to control your bladder, Bill thought with crazy gaiety—and then the realization of where he was and what he'd done and had to do came over him and once more he was sober.

Bill stooped down over his victim and rolled him over onto his back. For a moment he stared down at him. He couldn't believe his luck. God, what a break! This was the man. To make sure Bill took the photograph from his pocket and checked. There wasn't any doubt. To make doubly sure, though, he went

48

through the man's pockets, found a letter. The name was the right one. There wasn't any doubt at all. This was the man.

Only, he was alive.

Unconscious, badly hurt perhaps, the little man on the floor wasn't dead. Bill looked at him and all his elation died. He couldn't kill that man. It was okay beating someone senseless in a boxing ring, in fact it was fun. And it was all very well bashing a shape on the head with a stick when your safety hung on it. Maybe he could even kill at a distance with a rifle which would be nice and impersonal. But here, the man was helpless. Small. He could even see his face. He didn't want to see that face.

All at once Bill decided to get the hell out.

And then three things happened at exactly the same time: he realised that his face had been seen; there was the sound of fresh footsteps in the passageway; the man on the floor began to moan.

Bill stared at him in horror. He lifted the stick again—the footsteps were coming this way. He couldn't do it. The footsteps. The man was making a noise. He had to stop that noise. He had a desperate inspiration. He dragged his semi-conscious victim across the floor to the toilet and held his face down in the bowl. No one could make a noise with his face under water! Just for a second. Till the footsteps have gone.

The man became more conscious then and jerked to get away. Don't! Please! *Don't do that!* Bill prayed. And exerted more strength. And he was strong. And held the man down. And after a while he didn't make any noise anymore.

Bill let him go. Outside the toilet door there was silence. Bill straightened.

"Stephen? Everything all right?"

It was a woman's voice from the other side of the door. It came so sharp and sudden that Bill felt his heart lurch out of place in his chest.

"Stephen?"

But Bill had just made sure that Stephen would never speak again. He stood there for a frozen second of eternity. Then he

49

thought of turning on the basin tap. He did. The noise reassured the woman.

"Well, hurry up now. Coffee's getting cold!"

Bill heard her footsteps receding down the passage. What sort of bitch would nag her husband even in the john, he wondered. Maybe the man was well rid of her. Bill looked across at him. Oh God, he was rid of everything. Lolling there. Quite still.

Bill reeled away and opened the door. Then he remembered the stick and picked it up and took it with him out into the hall and put it back in the stand. There was no one in the hall and he went out unmolested.

He managed to get to the rhododendrons before he was sick.

On the way back to London, Bill began to feel better. The further he got from the house the better he felt. It had been a gruesome experience but he'd done it. That had taken guts. And anyhow, it was done. Over. Forever. He'd worn gloves all night, hadn't left a fingerprint or a clue. He was safe. And now he was going to get paid. Five godlike grand! That was money. The whole world opened up with that kind of cash in your hand.

Bill was calm and almost smiling as he got to London and abandoned the stolen car.

As an offering to other would-be car thieves, he left the keys in the ignition where he'd found them. Then he caught a bus. It wasn't that late and he saw no reason why he shouldn't go and collect right away.

The house of his old school friend was in central London in an exclusive residential square. It was just after eleven when Bill walked down its tree-lined pavements up to the steps of the house and rang the bell. The windows of the house were in darkness and for a moment Bill thought his friend might be out. But he leant on the bell awhile and was pleased to see a light come on and then to hear footsteps approaching the door.

It was opened by a stooping middle-aged man in a dark butler's uniform. "Yes?" he demanded—rather severely, Bill thought for a servant.

"I'd like to see Mr. Bertram."

50

"Mr. Bertram is not at home," the butler replied frostily. But his lie fell flat for even as he finished speaking, Bill heard the voice of Bertie himself calling, "Who the hell's that, Charles?"

"Bill Armstrong, Bertie!" Bill called, pushing past the butler into the house. There were stairs facing him and at the top of them was his friend—with half-unbuttoned shirt which clearly announced he'd been undressing for bed.

"What brings you here at this time of night?" he mumbled.

"Sorry to disturb you"—Bill smiled up at him—"but there's something you ought to know."

"Now?"

"*Right* now."

"Oh. Yeah. Better come up then."

Bill went up the stairs to the first floor and followed his host into a study. It was a sumptuous lived-in room with silk-lined walls, shelves of leather-bound volumes and a marble fireplace in which a fire still smouldered. Bertie went to the fire, stood with his back to it, leaned on the mantlepiece with an elbow and stared at Bill nervously.

"Well?"

Bill studied him. Apart from losing some hair, the man hadn't really changed since school at all. He still looked pallid, thin—a weed.

"Sorry to keep you from your cot," Bill said gaily, "but I've got some news that won't wait."

Bertie smiled superciliously. "You are drunk are you?"

Bill's eyes narrowed. "No. I'm not."

"Sorry. Just kidding. Use one now?" Without waiting for a reply, Bertie moved to a wall and pressed a bell. He turned back towards Bill and smiled. "Right," he went on, "tell all."

"I attended to that little matter for you," Bill told him.

"What?"

Bill began to lose patience. What was the moron playing at, he wondered. He'd been through enough already this evening without these games.

"A few days ago," he replied, "you offered me five thousand to . . . dispose of some rubbish for you. I'm here to collect."

51

As Bill finished speaking Bertie's anaemic face went more bloodless still. He looked at Bill piercingly. "You're pulling my leg!"

"If I am, the joke's a pretty sick one. Especially for someone called Stephen. It's so sick for him, he's dead."

There was a knock on the study door. Automatically Bertie said, "Come!" and the butler entered the room carrying a silver tray with drinks. With ponderous slowness he crossed the room, placed the tray on a table by the fire, checked that everything on it was in order.

"Will there be anything else, sir?" he asked at last, turning to his employer.

"No, thank you, Charles," Bertie replied, still staring fixedly at Bill.

"Very good, sir. Good night." And the butler left.

Bertie took his eyes from Bill's face then and poured himself a large brandy. "What'll you have?" he asked over his shoulder.

"Whisky and water, please."

Bertie poured. "So you really did it?" he almost stated as he turned back and handed Bill the drink.

"Yes."

"Were there . . . any problems?"

"No."

"He's dead."

"Yes."

"Are you quite sure?"

"Absolutely."

"No doubt at all?"

"None at all, I'm telling you. You want the bloody details?"

"No. I think you can spare me that."

Bill looked at his friend closely and noticed that though he'd spoken coolly the colour was in his cheeks and his eyes were bubbling with an excitement he seemed to find hard to control.

"Well, well," he started to chuckle, "no more Stephen! Good for you, lad!" And Bertie raised his glass to Bill in a toast and drank deep. Finishing his drink, he put down his glass and smiled. "Splendid. And I'm really glad you came and told me.

Really glad. Still—life has to go on and I've had a pretty tiring day so now, if you'll excuse me, I think I'll get to bed." He began to move towards the door. "Do stay and finish your drink, though, by all means."

For a moment Bill stood dazed. Then he moved. Fast. He just reached the door of the room before his friend and, turning his back to it, stood blocking the way. Bertie looked at him with a frown.

"Isn't there something you've forgotten?" Bill asked him quietly.

"Forgotten?"

Bill looked down at Bertie and his mind went glacially cold. You've got a nerve, he thought—now that the job's done, trying to get out of paying. Little swine. I remember taking the pants off you in the locker-rooms. Who do you think you're trying to fool?

"There's a little matter of cash, man."

"Oh—*that!*" Bertie's tone was contemptuous. "You needn't worry. You'll be paid, I assure you."

Bertie tried to move round Bill to get out the door, but Bill moved also and blocked him.

"I think now's as good a time as any, don't you?" Bill said gently.

Bertie looked at him superciliously. "You must be joking. I don't keep anything like that sort of money here!"

For an instant the sincerity, the scorn the words carried almost deceived him—but then Bill remembered the size of the wad from which Bertie had peeled off his "advance" and he realised with grim certainty that his friend was trying to con him. His lips moved back in a sneer as he said, "I'll take what you have. You can owe me the rest."

Bertie looked up at the bigger, heavier man blocking his exit from the room and for just a second Bill wondered if he was going to try something, but all he said was "Very well," and turned away. Bill watched him as he moved across to a bookshelf by the fire and withdrew fat volumes. Behind them, at head height, was a safe. Bertie began to play the dial. He

53

gave in pretty easily, Bill thought—too easily he realised with a chill of intuition—and began to move across the room towards his friend. As he did so, the combination clicked, the tiny door swung open, Bertie's whole body tensed with purpose.

Bill sprang. So fast that he managed to clear the distance between him and Bertie while his friend was still tensed to act—and even before Bertie could get a hand to the safe Bill had driven his clubbed fist into the back of his neck.

Bertie's head cannoned forward into the safe. And stuck there.

Bill leapt back, ready to meet resistance. But there wasn't any. Bertie was unconscious, his head jammed fast. Bill rubbed his knuckles and looked at it and began to laugh. Still laughing, he reached out and took hold of his friend's thin hair—and pulled. He had to tug quite hard before the head came away and the body slumped to the floor.

Bill looked into the safe. And all his amusement died and the skin prickled cold down his spine. Butt facing towards him was the oiled gleam of a Mauser. Safety-catch off. Bill looked at it. It didn't have a very wide barrel, but he reckoned it made a big enough hole. Could Bertie have been going to use that? The mental question never got answered. For he saw what was beside the gun.

Wads.

Five neat, rubber-banded wads. Of money. The stuff of life! Bill looked at them and everything went out of his mind in the wonder of them. Slowly, almost reverently, he put a hand into the safe and drew them out. They felt the best thing he'd ever held. He took them to a table a little way from the fire and sat down in a chair by it and put each wad separately on the table. He looked across towards the safe. Bertie was lying, apparently unconscious, beneath it but the gun was still there. Not the cleverest place to leave it, Bill thought, and he got up and took it out. He handled it gingerly as he did so, was careful to put on the safety-catch before picking it up. He'd never held an automatic before, but was surprised that, once it was in his hand, it seemed to nestle there as naturally as a knife in its sheath.

He went back, put the gun on the table, and began to count

the money. He had counted just one bundle when he was conscious that Bertie was coming round. He looked across at him. He was leaning groggily against the wall now, rubbing his head. He looked at Bill with an expression of little love.

"That was silly of you, Bertie." Bill smiled at him, gesturing with his gun towards the safe.

But, whether from pain or anger, Bertie did not reply.

"Come on now, lad," Bill said sympathetically. "Sorry about the head 'n' all, but you'd better get a grip on yourself, because you and I are going to have to talk."

Bill stood. He picked up the gun and worked the chamber till he'd ejected all the bullets from the magazine onto the table, then he put down the gun and strolled across to Bertie. He helped him off the floor and into an arm-chair by the fire.

"That *was* a bloody silly thing to do, you know," he said.

He went to the drink tray and poured out a brandy and handed it to the man in the chair. Bertie took it sullenly. "We had a gentleman's agreement on this thing," Bill said kindly. "You can't walk out on it now."

Bertie swallowed a mouthful of his drink and looked up at Bill viciously. "Oh can't I!"

"No."

"Oh no? Well what if I went to the police and told them you did it?"

Bill went and poured himself a whisky. "That'd be fine. But how come *you* know that? And what motive have *I* for killing a man I've never met? On the other hand, though, I suspect *you* have a motive, Bertie." Bill drank, stared at his friend over the glass, watched his colour deepen in anger. "Ah you do!" he said, settling on the arm of a chair near Bertie's. "A good one, I'm sure. And—here's a strange coincidence: I just happen to have the man's name and address in your handwriting and his photograph with your fingerprints all over it. Oh, they might get me, but, if they did, I'd certainly get you. So, you see, there's nothing to stop your going to the police, lad. But if you did, the throat you cut would be your own."

Bertie looked at Bill with hatred and anger, but unable to dispute the logic of what he had said, he took another drink.

"It'd be a lot easier just to pay me what you owe me," Bill said.

Bertie got to his feet. The brandy had given him back some courage. He came and stood over Bill and spat out: "You've got no way of making me pay!"

Bill stood. "No way at all," he agreed sadly and hit Bertie precisely in the solar plexus.

Bertie doubled up winded onto his knees on the floor. Bill looked down at him an instant, then swiftly and not gently at all he heaved him off the floor and dumped him back in the chair from which he'd just risen. Bertie slumped there on his side, sobbing and gasping to breath.

"Be sensible," Bill told him coldly. "An agreement's an agreement. I've kept my side of our bargain and you're going to keep yours. Whether you like it or not."

Bill turned away and went back to the table where he had left the money. "Bertie!" he ordered sharply and, despite his pain, the tone of Bill's voice was such that Bertie looked up and nodded—a child submissive to the voice of authority.

"How much is this little lot?" Bill asked indicating the notes.

"Two thousand, two hundred," Bertie managed to gasp.

"Good. A convenient sum. Counting the three hundred advance you paid me, that comes to exactly half." Bill began to disperse the money between his jacket and trousers. It made the well-tailored pockets bulge. When he had it all put away, he looked across at his friend, who had managed to get to a sitting position in the chair.

"I think there's something you ought to realise, Bertie," Bill said and took the automatic from the table and removing its magazine began to feed back the bullets. "I am no longer the good old Bill Armstrong you were at school with. Thanks to you, I am now a murderer." Bill finished loading the magazine and now slipped it back into the gun. It went home with an oiled click and as he looked at the gun in Bill's hand and heard that sound, Bertie's face went chalk pale.

"Yes," Bill went on, bringing up the gun, "a murderer. Not the sort of man you mess around."

Bertie's face was drawn with fear, his lips pulled back from his teeth and his mouth opened but no words came.

"I'm going to return in a couple of weeks and I want my money ready. Do you understand?"

Bertie nodded.

"Good." Bill smiled. He waved the gun. "In the meantime I think I'll have to confiscate this. It looks dangerous." He walked to the door, turned for a final word. "You know, I'm disappointed in you, Bertie. You should be paying me double out of gratitude—not fiddling around over a few paltry grand. See you!" And Bill gave a wave and left.

Outside, in the peaceful London square, Bill stood for a moment remembering the conversation and he couldn't help but grin as he thought of the fear his friend had shown when he levelled the gun. He'd get his money all right. He took a deep contented breath and began to walk away.

The cold night air felt good and clean on his face.

Bill lived by the river in a neighbourhood a long way in distance and even further in style from that of his friend. Despite the distance he decided to take a cab home. Right now he could afford it.

It was one o'clock when Bill finally stood on the steps of his apartment and looked across the street-lamped road to the oiled gleam of the river at night. The sight always chilled him. It was a swirling shroud over eternally sunless muds and ooze. It had depths of blackness that could stretch right down to hell. A good place for the gun to go, Bill decided, becoming conscious of the tug of it in his pocket. He crossed the road and threw it far out to the river. It met the water with only a slight splash and then was gone without ripples. Over the timeless time that the river had been there, Bill wondered how many corpses had gone down that way. Not his at least—and he crossed back and went down the steps to his basement flat. As he took out his keys, he heard the moan of a police siren in the distance. For a moment it froze him. But then, as it began to die, he realised it was not coming for him, nor could be. He looked at his hand stretched out with key to the lock. Black gloves. He'd worn them all night. Left no clues. There's a lot a man can do, he reflected as he turned the key, with nerve and a good pair of gloves.

Taking care to be quiet, he let himself into the flat. Immediately he opened the door he could smell the damp of it. The lights were off but even in the dark the place breathed slum. Still, he thought, there'd be better things from now on. Without turning on the lights, Bill felt his way through the dilapidated entrance room into the adjoining bedroom. Though he couldn't see her, he knew that Sylvia was asleep in the small double bed. She was snoring. Bill stood and listened. It wasn't a romantic sound. Imagine, he thought with surprise, I've spent all those nights beside *that*. It was like being next to a snoring sow. Well, not quite. Bill's eyes were more accustomed to the dark now and he could see the outline of Sylvia's body in the bed. No sow had a shape like that! He walked past her quietly, went through into the next-door bathroom, locked its door behind him, and turned on the light.

Home.

He felt great. Tired now, but great. He put the plug in the bath, started running the water—and caught sight of himself in a full-length mirror. Wavy dark hair, liquid sensitive brown eyes, manly chin—he liked what he saw. He removed his jacket, took the money from its pockets, stacked it neatly on a stool by the bath. He took off the rest of his clothes and examined his naked body in the mirror with satisfaction. He was tall. His muscles taut. There wasn't an ounce of flab on him. You're a good-looking devil, Armstrong, he thought, and grinned and got into the bath.

He lay in the steaming water and looked at the holy money on the stool by the bath—and everything else went out of his mind. For a while he just stared at the money, savouring it. Then slowly, so as not to end the ecstasy too soon, he began to count it.

There was a lot to count.

All in crumpled fives, used, impossible to trace now. Alto-

58

gether there were five wads. Four held one hundred notes. One held forty. Though his maths had never been strong, it didn't take Bill long to total it all to two thousand two hundred. Exactly as Bertie had said.

Lying quite still in the bath with his hand dappling the money beside him, Bill Armstrong felt a calm and a confidence like he had never known. The night had changed him, he realised. Without ever consciously thinking, he knew decisions had been made in his mind. He had crossed bridges and could never go back. Things were clearer. He was more assured, perhaps more mature. He grinned a bit at that. Screw being mature. That was like being responsible. All he wanted was to be rich. And now he knew he would be and would never have to work in the conventional sense again. The night had been the start of a new way of life. Grinning, he got out of the bath. He wondered if his father would have been pleased to have known that after all this time, his son had at last found a "career."

Bill dried, bundled the money together, doused the light and slipped into the bedroom and bed. Sylvia gave a little moan as he got in beside her, then fell back to sleep and began to snore again. Bill kept still an instant, then slipped the money under his pillow. And within minutes slept the sound, childlike sleep of those healthy in mind and body and whose conscience is perfectly clear.

"So what time did you get in, then?"

The acid Australian voice woke him. He yawned and flexed and his hand slid under the pillow—and found the reassuring wads. He opened his eyes. Sylvia was propped up on an elbow looking down at him in the early morning light and beneath her very blond hair her unlined face was hard with a scowl.

"Well?"

Gosh, Bill noticed for the first time as he gazed up at her, she wears her false eyelashes in bed! Then his eyes moved down to where her breasts were mushrooming up through her nightdress and he felt a bit dizzy. The sight of them never failed to get him. They were one of the wonders of the world!

"Answer me, blast you!"

Ha! Bill thought, Mr. Heffner and others whose fortunes had been founded on exposure of the female form might think they'd seen some pretty fine specimens, but they'd have blown their minds if they could have seen Sylvia now.

"Answer me!" she screamed.

In way of answer Bill reached out his arms to her—wishing with part of his mind even as he did so that she didn't have that awful Australian accent. It was enough to put a man off.

"No you bloody don't!" Sylvia jerked back from his hands. "Just who do you think you are?"

She spat on. But Bill ceased to listen. Instead he just lay and looked at her and for the first time in their relationship felt totally in command and assured. For a while he let his eyes take in how splendid she looked in her anger. Then he reached under his pillow and detached a thick handful of notes from the wad. Without a word he held them out to her and her eyes widened and her yammering abruptly stopped.

"Be quiet now, will you, love," he ordered tolerantly and lifted the hand with the money in it over her and slowly, one by one, let the notes flutter down onto her body.

And this time she didn't move away from his hands.

"I'm sorry I was angry," she told him some time later. "It's only that I care for you . . . so much."

Sylvia lay beside him, nuzzling the side of his face. Bill lay on his back, hands behind his head, at ease. He waited without replying for the question he guessed would soon come. It did. Almost at once.

"Were you gambling last night?"

Bill turned his head and looked at her. The power of money was fantastic. Not very long ago her face had been screwed into shrewish rage. Now it was watching him with dewy-eyed, frank adoration. Funny that he'd wanted this girl so much. So much that he'd even killed for her. No. That wasn't true. He hadn't done it for her. Perhaps to be able to have what it took to have her—or someone like her—but not for her.

"Yeah," he replied.

60

"Uh—how did you do?" she smiled at him tentatively.

Dumb cow, Bill thought, smiling back at her. I go and shower her with bread and she asks how I've done!

"Not badly," he answered.

"How—how much did you win, darling?"

Bill shrugged and said casually: "Oh, about two and a half grand or so."

Sylvia's eyes flared. Bill imagined he could hear cash-registers clinking behind them. She'd got an adding-machine for a mind, he thought, and it's going berserk. For a moment she was speechless. Then she whispered, "Oh, I'm so glad for you!"

She began to kiss him. He let her for a time, for a time took the avarice of her mouth on his lips. Then he pushed her away. Her magic had gone. Her kisses did nothing for him now and he knew that everything he'd ever felt for her was dead. It was time to move on.

"Go and get me a paper, love, will you?" he told her.

Almost at once she rose from the bed. "Your wish, master, is my command!" She smiled at him. Going to a cupboard, she took out tight sweater, tenuous skirt, began to wriggle into them. Dressed, she came back, kissed him. "Won't be a jiff," she chirped. And went out to get the newspaper.

The second the door slammed behind her, Bill rose. He scooped the cash from under his pillow, took a briefcase from beneath the bed, arranged the money in it in neat blue rows—and smiled down at them paternally. Then he padded into the entrance/living room. Furniture was beaten and ragged, wallpaper dirty, flaked, in places dark with damp. How sick, Bill thought, that a man with his background should have sunk to this hovel. Still—it had served its purpose and soon he would leave it and all that it stood for behind. For good.

He went to a chest of drawers. Somewhere in here, he knew, Sylvia had a hiding place. He opened the drawers and began to rummage through them. It didn't take much finding. It was at the back of the bottom drawer concealed behind a pile of dirty clothes. Her jewel-box.

He took it out and opened it. The stuff inside was hardly worth a fortune. Bill knew because he'd bought it for her, but it might be useful for the next bird and besides, having given it, he felt he had it coming back. So he took the cheap jewellery that he'd once presented her with so much show of love and put it in his dressing-gown pocket. And that was all there was in the box. Till he noticed that it had a false bottom and in a hidden compartment beneath the jewels was a shelf holding passport and letters and a nice thick bundle of Australian dollars. Bill glanced at the passport photo—God, she looked a joke! Then he began to read through the letters.

He didn't read very far. They were letters from the mother and family that Sylvia had left behind—simple letters written with love and the sense of loss. The money, he realised, was Sylvia's insurance. Enough to pay for her flight back home. It was a healthy sum, a sum he could use. But seeing it there beside the letters, he saw Sylvia—not as a steely, urbane exploiter, but as a young girl just trying to get on, a long way from home—and he pitied her. He tried to put the feeling behind him. Pity, he knew, never got a man anywhere.

But he left the return-fare money in the jewel-box just the same.

He replaced the box, took its former contents back and added them to the money in the briefcase, which he locked and slid back under the bed. Where would she have put the cash he'd recently scattered on top of her, he wondered. In her handbag most likely and she'd taken that with her. Still, there'd be time for that later on. He got back into bed.

Sylvia returned with the paper, gave it to him with a kiss and, because they didn't have a kitchen, went into the bathroom to make coffee.

Bill scanned the paper for mention of his feat last night. He was a little disappointed to find that there wasn't any, but consoled himself with the thought that they must have gone to press before the news got out.

Sylvia reappeared with coffee. "What shall we do today, doll?" she asked, handing it to him and puffing up the pillows behind his back.

"Lunch in the country, maybe. Then—some shopping, maybe a movie . . ." He looked away. He was sorry he had to deceive her but he didn't see he had any choice.

She grinned at him. "That'd be *fab!*"

"Right!" he went on. "Run me a bath, do yourself up—and we'll split!"

He turned his attention to the paper and she scurried to obey. He finished his coffee, got out of bed, put on his dressing-gown again and loped into the bathroom. She was kneeling by the bath with her back to him, swishing the water to get it at an even temperature. Her handbag was slung over her shoulder. Bill got down behind her, wrapped an arm round her and started to kiss the back of her neck. She went obligingly limp in his arms.

"Can't get enough, can you?" she giggled as she turned her face towards him.

It wasn't difficult to undo her bag, remove the money and transfer it to his dressing-gown pocket. After which he closed the bag and involved himself in the embrace. She noticed nothing.

"Whew!" he exclaimed, pulling back from her. "We'll never get anywhere at this rate! I'll take my bath now and—look, be a love and just slip over to Sulka's and pick up some shirts I've had made, could you?"

"All rightie!" She pecked his cheek, rose and began to repair her hair in front of a mirror. Bill got into the bath.

"Why don't you take a cab while you're at it?" he suggested.

"Will do, lover." She smiled at him. And swayed away.

"See you!" he called after her. Then felt a bit strange. Because he knew that he'd never see her again.

When he heard her close the front door, he got out of the bath and went to work. Fast. He dried and dressed in a conservative, tailor-made suit. Unpaid for. But safely because the tailors had dressed his family for generations and weren't troublesome over debts. Next, he got out his two monogrammed pigskin suitcases and quickly and methodically packed. Within fifteen minutes he was out of the flat—having stripped it of everything he owned. It wasn't much—enough to fill two cases —and all of it clothes. Immaculate clothes. That was all.

He shut the apartment door, conscious that he was shutting a door in his life behind him, and went up the stairs without looking back and without a pang.

His grey Aston Martin was parked across the road by the river. He carried his luggage across to it. As usual there was a parking ticket stuck to its windscreen. Bill detached it, dropped it into the gutter; placed his cases in the car. Just about now, he reckoned, Sylvia would be getting out of her cab. She'd open her handbag —and find the money he'd given her gone. Would she catch on right away? Or would she think she'd left it in his flat and go into the shop anyhow to ask for his never-ordered shirts? Either way he'd never know the answer. When she got back, he'd be long, long gone.

He jumped into the car, started the engine, punched on the slot-stereo, started humming with the Stones. Maybe it wasn't the kindest way to say good-bye, he thought, but at least she's going to get the message. He smiled. A little wryly. Then he drove away.

It was just after ten o'clock when he reached Victoria Station; parked neatly on a double no-parking line; carried in his cases and, apart from the money-filled briefcase, which he kept in his hand, deposited them in the left-luggage.

Then he joined the line outside the ticket office.

The decision had been formed in the night by his subconscious mind and crystallised when he woke. Now he was acting on it. It was time to get away. Not to run from the law—he'd left no clues and they would never find him. No. It was just that the moment had come to move on for a while. To greener pastures. To take a break. The place to be at this time of the year anyhow was the South of France and for the first time he could afford to go there. It would only be for two weeks. Then he'd come back and collect the rest of his money. But meanwhile the weather would be great; the big bread would be making itself felt round the gaming tables of Monte Carlo; there'd be plenty of scope for a man of his talents.

Bill bought a first-class ticket on the Golden Arrow—due to depart in half an hour.

Coming out of the station, he bought another paper, glanced quickly through it, but still could find no mention of the murder. It was worrying. Lousy reporters ought to be shot, he thought, moving to his car. And then he saw a policeman by it, writing out a ticket. For a moment he paused in his stride. Then he went smoothly up to the man, took the ticket, thanked him, got into the car and drove off. To a nearby garage. Here he saw the Aston safely stabled; gave the man instructions to look after it and a healthy tip. For a moment, then, he lingered by the car. He loved this machine and hated to be parted from it. He knew though that French roads would play havoc with its hard suspension—and that if he ever had a breakdown, he'd never get spares. Consoling himself with the thought that he'd only be parted from the car for two weeks, he turned and went back to the station.

Of course he could always have jetted to the South of France in a matter of hours. But he preferred a train journey: it offered more leisure, more comfort than a plane. And when it came down to it, he was frightened of flying.

So it was that, at ten-fifteen on Friday the twenty-fourth of September in the year of Our Lord 1971, Bill Armstrong, recently turned killer for cash, arrived back at Victoria Station; took his cases from the left-luggage; and strolled onto platform eight.

Without a care in this world.

CHAPTER 4

SUITCASE in hand, Bill Armstrong moved up the corridor of the train, looking in at the compartments. They were full or filling and he saw he was lucky to have got a place at such short notice—or would be, if he could only find it. He had walked all the way from the back of the train and was now nearly at the front, but so far had failed to locate his place among the few reserved seats. He was in the last carriage before the engine now, and if it wasn't here it wouldn't be anywhere.

It was.

Pinned above the white antimacassar on the head-rest of the blue high-pile seat immediately by a compartment door, Bill saw the well-loved word. Armstrong.

He slid back the door, entered the compartment. It was empty; looked neat and oddly new and unused. For an irretrievable moment Bill paused on the threshold. For a second, felt strangely uncomfortable that on such a crowded train there should be this one quite empty compartment—and he should be in it. But then he noticed that the other seats were also reserved; and he stepped in and slid shut the door behind him and swung his cases to the rack. Unthinkingly, he reached to put his briefcase up alongside them. Then he remembered the money that was in it and drew it back and held it close to him as he sat down. With over two grand, he thought, one just couldn't be too careful: the world was full of thieves.

Bill sat loosely, looked loosely round the compartment, but his hand was tight on his briefcase and he felt on edge. He glanced without purpose at his watch, swung his feet up onto the seat in front of him, swung them down again. He was twitchy. Maybe it's this lousy seat, he thought. Nearest the corridor, furthest from the window, back to the engine . . . they put people in seats like this, they ought to give them their money back. Abruptly, Bill got up; unpinned his name from above his place; was about to swap it with the name on the opposite window-seat when he saw three smart fawn cases established along the rack above. Damn! he thought, someone's already got there. Then he noticed the luggage was monogrammed "A.C." He checked the name on the window seat: "Dr. Latimer." That was all right. Then he checked the other names: "Rev. Staymore," another "Latimer"—"Miss" this time—a blank, and a "Miss Cross." "C"—that was it. No problem. Her place was on the opposite row, one away from the window.

Bill contentedly completed the change-round of his own and Doctor Latimer's name, moved his bags down the rack, put his briefcase on the floor by his feet, and relaxed in his new seat.

He felt better right away. He'd achieved something! And the window-seat gave him a feeling of command over the rest of the compartment. Then he began to wonder about the Miss Cross who owned the luggage. Maybe he'd been wrong to have moved from his original seat, where she'd have been right beside him —she might have turned out to be a gorgeous dolly dying to chat up a man! Sure. So might Miss Latimer, whom he'd be sitting next to this side. For a moment he had a vision of an unbelievably beautiful woman cuddling next to him with her head on his shoulder and gazing up at his face with adoration. He grinned. That wouldn't do the journey any harm at all, he thought, and turned his face and looked out the window to watch the activity on the station platform.

He was watching it as Ann Cross came back into the compartment. Her entrance was muffled by the sound of a leaving train and Bill didn't notice her. But almost before she had closed the door behind her, she had assessed him. With the eye of one whose business was people she took in his parts and they gave the score of him whole. Weak mouth, strong jaw, tailor-made suit, silk shirt, clothes expensive but quiet: probable character, basically self-indulgent but controlled; occupation, middle-weight executive of some kind; background, educated, with a little money.

Summation—no use to her at all.

All this went through her mind as her eyes slid once over Bill Armstrong and she shut the door and took her seat.

She looked at him for one moment more. Perhaps some years ago this man might have been able to help her. Not today.

Bill sensed her presence and turned his face from the window. Ann did not drop her eyes before his quick, measuring stare. He smiled at her.

"Morning!" he said.

She did not reply. Her face did not change expression. She gazed away past Bill out the window.

A cool-enough piece, he thought. Not bad-looking. But he was in the right seat after all. There wouldn't have been any great romance with this one. But almost opposite her here, he could at least stare her down. And those legs were worth a look. Too bad her skirt was so long . . .

Quite suddenly all thoughts of female charms were wiped from his mind—by the sight of a huge, heavily fat, black-robed priest squeezing through the door into the compartment. For a moment Bill gaped at him with simple revulsion. Then something clicked in his brain and he wondered if he could ever stop a man like that with his hands. It wouldn't be something he'd like to try, he decided. He imagined his right jabbing short and hard to the priest's solar plexus. The blow would be useless; his arm sunk into flab almost up to the elbow—all the force absorbed. The man was probably mammothly strong, too. Bill had a vision of those immense grey hands slowly closing round his windpipe and inexorably tightening. No. The only way to fight this man would be to go for the eyes—and go fast. Or maybe below the belt . . .

"Good morning," said the Reverend Sullivan Staymore.

"Good morning, Father," Ann Cross replied.

"Morning!" Bill contributed—then suddenly smiled. "Father!" he thought. Of course. How dumb can you get? There wasn't any danger that he'd ever conceivably have to battle with this monument of a man.

"Lovely day, isn't it?" Bill added cheerfully.

The words were addressed chiefly to Ann but she had started to read her business journal and made no effort to answer and it was Staymore who replied.

"Indeed. Indeed."

Staymore placed a modest zipper bag in the rack, gathered his robes around himself in preparation to sit. Bill partially turned his face to the window, but watched him out of the side of his eyes. He was directly opposite. Right by the woman. Bill could see that, though ostensibly she was engrossed in her magazine, the huge physical presence of the man was making her uncomfortable and she was edging down the seat away from him.

Staymore sat. Amused, Bill noticed the woman shift quickly still further away. She had to. The priest's bulk flowed out over a place and a half. If he'd remained in his original seat, Bill saw he'd have been pleasantly crushed against her. Oh well . . . no one could win them all.

But as Bill continued to watch the couple opposite, he saw he hadn't lost out at all.

The priest now held an open breviary and was concentrating at it—his lips, faintly specked with saliva, moving in silent recitation. The woman too was attempting to involve herself in reading. But not so successfully. Looking at the grotesque figure beside her, Bill understood why. The man's bristled face was sparkling with sweat, his white priest's collar limp with it. "B.O." just wasn't the word, Bill thought wryly. Not all the Lifebuoy in the wide dry antiperspirant world could ever cope with what oozed from those pallid pores. Bill got the whiff of it loud and clear some feet away and he figured that sitting there next to him must be like snuggling up to a nice ripe garbage can—on a sweltering day.

The woman obviously thought so too. Her lips were slightly open, as if she'd been trying to breathe through her mouth rather than her nose, but it wasn't working. Now she looked deliberately up from her magazine at the priest and her face creased with distaste.

But his breviary was a blanket against the world and he read on unaware.

Bill looked openly at the two of them and openly grinned. Then he relaxed in his seat, slid back the narrow upper segment of the window by which he sat, conspicuously inhaled the fresh air that blew on his face—and happily sighed out loud.

Ann Cross noted his performance and wasn't amused. She rose. Detaching her name from her seat, she stepped gracefully across the compartment to the corridor-seat on Bill's side. The name-space above it was blank. Ann pinned her name there and sat. Staymore had not looked up.

Bill swivelled to face her. "You sure you wouldn't rather sit here by the window?" he offered, mocking and cavalier.

Ann looked at him; made a smile shape with her mouth. She spoke so flat the words meant nothing. "You're too kind," she replied.

"Not at all!"

"I'm fine right here."

"Oh. Well, suit yourself."

They looked into each other's eyes. Looked deep. Neither even pretended to smile. You're a tough nut, Bill thought; God, I'd like to crack you! The thought provoked a vision. In it, his hand was huge. Her head a brittle shell. His hand closed over it. There were maggots inside.

Bill looked quickly away out the window. He wished he hadn't thought that. Wriggling slimy things made his stomach squirm. He hated even threading a worm on a fish-hook. Blast her!

So much for him, Ann thought as Bill looked away. She hadn't expected him to last long before his will gave in to hers and she stared him down. She'd often noticed that the tougher a man looked the weaker he was and in her experience this mocking rather muscular type was an elephant in ego all right, but when it came to guts, was a mouse. This one was clearly no exception. She dropped Bill in a mental trash-can and settled down to her magazine.

The Reverend Sullivan Staymore's eyes flicked up from his breviary. They stabbed towards the woman. The power of the word of God amazed him. She had been unable to even sit next to it. Evil. She must be evil. But then, weren't all women? For were they not the instrument of man's fall from Paradise? Yes. It was a cause of wonder to him how, out of all the ways the Redeemer could have chosen to come, he elected to be born of woman. In Staymore's mind, it was His greatest sacrifice.

He switched his eyes from the woman to the man.

A nice-looking young man, Staymore thought, and correctly dressed—an achievement itself in this peacock age. His features were well born, too, composed and serene. Staymore's incisive glance could see at once that this was a moderate, balanced man —at peace with himself and the world. And peace he knew was the gift of the pure in heart. Yes, this was a gentle man. It showed. In the soft, compassionate lips, the warm and understanding eyes. The eyes which were turning towards him even now and into which he was smiling.

After a moment, the young man smiled back. A little shyly perhaps, but nonetheless, Staymore thought, with a very nice smile.

The time was ten twenty-five.

Ann Cross was reading her magazine. The Reverend Sullivan

71

Staymore was admiring Bill Armstrong. Bill was forcing himself to smile politely into the priest's pellet eyes.

This was the moment the Latimers came through the door.

As they did so, Staymore dropped his gaze to his breviary. Ann Cross went on reading without looking up. Only Bill turned to look at the newcomers.

Doctor Latimer came in first. He was carrying a shabby suitcase and the classic doctor's bag. He was middle-sized, late middle-aged, nondescript. With a bland, instantly forgettable face. He looked like anyone and no one. He had only two even slightly distinguishing features: heavy nicotine stains on stubby long-nailed fingers and, showing clear through wispy grey hair, a mottled pink skull like the shell of a crab.

But if Dr. Latimer was not remarkable, his daughter was.

She had thick long glowing hair. Violently black. It hung past her shoulders in folds of night. It wreathed around her thin, stretched, chalk-like face. A face with the scantest eyebrows, the palest lips, the whitest roundest most unfocused eyes that Bill had ever seen.

Well—he thought—that's it. His neighbour on the journey. It seemed pretty clear as he looked at her that his fantasy had been just that and this trip wasn't going to set up any milestones in his love-life.

The startling-looking girl who moved to sit beside him was no more than ten years old.

CHAPTER 5

AT the age of ten Felicity Latimer was sensitive. And her senses were such as most people never develop in a lifetime. As she followed the tweed-suited figure of her father into the compartment, they made the thin hairs along her spine start cold.

Evil.

It pulsed at her, as she entered, so heavy that for an instant she felt dizzy and wanted to clutch to the sliding door and close her eyes. She could sense it purring catlike round her; feel the velvet of it nuzzling her cheeks and the base of her neck. She opened all her eyes then and saw it batting out in black waves from the two men and the woman there. She had never known such aggregation of evil before. Her heart beat to it with an excitement that was as near as her pre-pubescent body could come to lust.

There was nothing in life she loved so much.

It had been that way ever since she first heard the Voice. She must have been about seven years old then. It was before she saw the Reflections. And it wasn't them at all. Talk with them was like talk with people except that all of a sudden sometimes when you were saying something, they just melted and weren't there. No. The Voice was quite different. It came first of everything. It came from inside her head.

"Kill." It suddenly opened up and told her.

It was summer. Late morning. She was sitting out on the lawn in front of that part of the house where her father had his surgery. He was in it now and he was doing something with the maid, the one who was so thin, with the funny wobbly eyes and the grey skin. He had taken off her top and was looking at her chest. He turned round and gazed out across the lawn and saw Felicity staring at him. He looked at her. Then drew the blinds across the window.

Felicity's eyes wandered along up the house. It was a large square stone house like a big overturned box four storeys tall and many hundreds of years old. It had lots of rooms and long dark corridors to hide and stalk it. Felicity looked to a moss-thick corner. High up there, right at the top was where her mother had her rooms—the rooms in which she'd been an invalid for years . . .

That was when she heard the Voice.

She turned round to try to see where it came from. But there was no one out there on the lawn except her and her cocker-spaniel puppy and she knew it couldn't have been the dog.

"Kill!" it told her again.

And this time she knew where the Voice came from. She picked up her spaniel pup and held it in her lap and started to stroke its neck.

"Kill what?" she asked it all inside her.

"Who."

"All right, kill *who,* then?"

74

"Kill Mummy, silly!" it replied—and started to giggle.

Felicity thought about what the Voice had just said and very soon she was giggling too. Picking up her puppy, she got up and started to walk away across the lawn, she and the Voice laughing together. She walked till she came to the pond at the end of the lawn in front of the trees and she stood beside it and looked in it at herself mirrored along its dark water. With her black hair tied in a bow behind her, she looked quite tall and old holding the puppy there by the waters of the pond.

"Mummy! Yes. Goodie—that would be fun!"

The Voice twittered with agreement and began to chant:

> "Kill her! Kill her!
> Boil her up 'n' spill her
> Down the drain
> Bash out her brain
> And see if she'll get iller!"

"How? Tell how!"

"Yah boo—won't tell you!"

"C'mon!"

"Shan't."

"Shan't do it, then."

"Go on. Spoil sport!"

"I'm *not!*"

"You *are* . . . if you don't do it."

"Won't unless you tell me how."

"I'll give you a clue, all right?"

"Well . . . okay, then!"

"Here it is: rat-tit-ti-tat, curiosity killed the cat!" The Voice made a noise like sticking out its tongue. "Catch me! Catch me! You can't catch me!" And away it went skipping down a corridor of her mind.

"Hey!" she called after it. But it was gone.

Felicity stroking the fluffy head of her puppy, pouting into the pond and thinking about the Voice's last words. She couldn't work them out. Still, there wasn't any point in worrying about them. Not now, anyway. Life and all its games had to go on.

She put down the puppy, carefully away from the edge of the pond so it wouldn't fall in, then reached up and unknotted the big red ribbon that held her hair behind her neck. She looked at the puppy. It hadn't moved much from where she put it down. It was sniffing at the grass in front of it cautiously and peering round it with not very good-seeing eyes. It was young. And small. Felicity called to it. It had just learnt its name and it turned towards her and gambolled a little towards her on not so steady legs. She knelt down to it and stroked it and rolled it over onto its back on the grass. The dog didn't like that and tried to roll back onto its feet but she put her hand on it and pressed it down. She tied one end of her ribbon around its right back leg— and knotted it tight. The pup began to twist quite violently then and jerk and whine but she didn't have very much difficulty in getting hold of the left front leg and tying it securely to the right back one.

She looked towards the house. It was too far for anyone in it to see or hear what she was doing.

She picked the dog up. Very gently. Cradling it in her arms. With its two opposing legs knotted together, it formed a sort of lopsided ball. It was snatching at the cord around its legs now with its teeth. But they were small. And there was little strength in its jaws. Felicity ruffled behind its floppy ears. Then she held it up to her face and smiled at the look of helplessness about it and kissed it.

Then she threw it into the pond.

It squirmed and kicked with its free feet and jerked its body. It rolled from its back to its side to its front—unable to maintain any equilibrium. It splashed. It yelped.

But not for very long. For, though the pond was only a foot or so deep, that was quite deep enough.

Felicity stood looking into the water till the ripples growing out from it stilled. She smiled. If it's that easy with Mummy, she thought, there won't be any trouble at all. But she realised it wouldn't be anything like that easy. She could hardly just carry her mother down from her bed four storeys up in the house out here across the lawn and drown her. And even though her mum had been ill for almost as long as she could remember, she was still a lot stronger than Felicity herself. Frowning with concentration, she fished the dead puppy out of the water, retrieved her hair ribbon, then dropped the dog back in. It looked surprisingly skinny all wet and dead. She wondered vaguely if the goldfish would eat it. Smoothing out the wet ribbon, she started to put it back in her hair and walked back across the lawn towards the house. "Rat-tit-ti-tat, curiosity killed the cat" kept running through her brain.

She was so preoccupied that, when she reached the house, she nearly stumbled into her father without seeing him.

"People get hurt like that," he said, catching hold of her.

"Oh! Hello, Daddy."

"Hello yourself."

She looked at him and decided this was the moment to break it. "Daddy . . ." she started plaintively.

"Yes?"

"Jimmy fell in the pond."

"Oh yes?"

"He drowned."

"He what?"

"Drowned." Not sure how he'd take this news, she made her face go all solemn and sad.

"Oh. Oh dear." She was watching him closely, but couldn't be sure if he was looking grim—or really wanting to smile and hiding it.

"Still," he went on, "not to worry. I'll get you a new one."

"Will you really, Daddy? Will you really?" she said, excitedly thinking of accidents she could arrange for it.

"Of course I will, my angel," he replied. And he took her hand and together they walked in to lunch.

Felicity was happy. She always loved holding her father's hands. They were blotched and wrinkly—and just what she imagined the hands of a corpse must be like that had lain some time in the grave. She forgot about killing her mother.

Till after lunch.

She was sitting in the woods past the pond at the end of the lawn. It was dark and cool in there with trees in places corded so thick overhead that all you could see was just spikes of sky through their branches. She was watching with wonder the ivy twined around an oak tree. It's been killing that tree for hundreds of years, she thought admiringly, little by little over all that time strangling it, sucking the strength away, draining its life out . . .

"Dummy, dummy—can't kill Mummy!" the Voice was derisive, echoing—heard. And then gone.

Angry, Felicity got up. No rotten old Voice was going to poke fun at her anymore. She walked quickly back to the house, went into the kitchen, started to rummage through cupboards and drawers. It didn't take her long to find what she wanted. She took it out, felt the weight of it in her hand.

"And just what do you think you're doing with *that?*"

Felicity turned. Their maid was standing behind her frowning down at her. She tried to smile. It didn't work. The woman reached out and removed the knife she held in her hand.

"Carving knives are *not* for little girls to play with," the woman said sternly. She put it back in the drawer, closed it and turned and leaned against it as she looked down at Felicity. "Now you run along and amuse yourself somewhere else. I've got work to do here and I don't want *you* underfoot."

Felicity looked at the woman in silence. She tried her thing of imagining her all made of wax in her mind and melting and burning down and dribbling away—she stared at the maid hard and imagined it—but she only looked rather crossly back at the silent child and lifted a threatening hand.

"Scram!" she ordered.

With dignity, Felicity turned and walked slowly away. "Brat," she heard the maid scowl under her breath—and then she was out of the kitchen. Immediately out of it, she spun round and stood just behind the door, listening. The maid wouldn't be there all day, she figured. And when she'd left she could go back and collect the knife.

78

Felicity didn't have long to wait.

She heard the maid going out of one of the other doors and she slipped back into the kitchen. She went to the drawer and stared in at the knife. It was a large butcher's chopper. With a thick, dull-gleaming two-sided blade that narrowed triangularly to a tiny point. It was heavy and very sharp. Staring at it now, Felicity saw that it was really much too conspicuous to carry all the way through the house and up four flights of stairs. No. She needed something she could hide, so no one could stop and question her on her way to her mother's room. She selected an eight-inch meat skewer, tucked it under her sweater, and left the kitchen.

The main stair was in a large flag-stoned hall around which it rose steeply to the top of the house. Felicity was quite out of breath by the time she had climbed all the steps and stood on the final landing. She paused there, getting her breath, and went close to the banisters and looked down. She didn't put any weight against the banisters because they were rickety and could go at any minute, but she got as near as she could and looked over them. It was a long drop and, now as always looking from a height, Felicity got the urge to throw herself over, half-convinced she would fly and glide through the air. With a sigh she made herself turn away. She knew she wouldn't really fly but would fall hard to her death with a broken neck on the flagstones far below.

Felicity walked as quietly as she could down the long dark corridor towards her mother's bedroom. In the past she'd discovered that if she kept very close to the wall there were places where the floor-boards didn't creak at all—and she was able to reach the room with hardly any noise. She was glad of that for it meant that her mother would now get a shock when she suddenly knocked on the door. She did. Felicity could hear the sudden rustle of the bed-clothes, the surprised intake of breath; then the "Come in" with all surprise carefully controlled out of the voice.

Felicity didn't come in, though. She waited. She wanted the uncertainty to grow in her mother's mind. And she wanted to examine her weapon. She took it out and stared at it lovingly. It was a thin twisted rod of metal with a sharp point. It wasn't as stylish as the big butcher's knife—but it'd do the job just fine. The thing to do would be to drive it straight into her mother's throat . . .

"Come in!" the woman called out again—loud and a little angry.

"Mustn't keep Mummy waiting!" the Voice said, suddenly jumping up sprightly in her mind.

Felicity smiled and did a little curtsey to it—and holding the meat skewer behind her back, she walked through the door. She felt only excitement as she did so. The thrill of reaching the climax of a game. But no emotion—affection, hatred, bitterness, even dislike—towards the woman she had come to kill at all.

It was ironic.

For Felicity's mother was a volatile woman—and hatred was the mainspring of her emotional life. She hated her daughter and always had hated her, even as a foetus in the womb. She hated her husband.

It was only because she hated him so much that Felicity was alive at all.

She and Robert Latimer were cousins. They first met when she was nine months old. They met again when she was twenty-four. Wealthy. Wilful. She had decided on whim to call on her recently qualified doctor cousin—even though there was nothing wrong with her.

There soon was.

Dr. Latimer examined his patient thoroughly. Too thoroughly. And yet, for a medical man, surprisingly carelessly. For some weeks after her first visit to his surgery, Margaret returned. To tell him she was expecting his child.

One month after that, though neither of them had wanted to, they married.

Two months later, Margaret miscarried. But that was two months too late.

For both of them. For if their marriage started bad, it continued worse. Apart from blood, they had nothing in common.

80

Even the attraction that had initially joined them soon fell apart and in the growing monotony of their relationship, their feelings for each other faded into total disinterest. Till six months after Margaret's miscarriage, there was nothing between them at all.

Which was one of the reasons Margaret hated Robert Latimer.

There were others. She was an ambitious woman. Socially, financially. Now she had a husband, she wanted him to go far. But the furthest Dr. Latimer wanted to go was to the country, where he could settle down with an easy established practice. And that's where they went. Here, Margaret used her money to buy a house and staff which, partially at least, served to gratify her need for status. But again her husband thwarted her by using the house as a surgery and filling it with the sick and socially undesirable towards whom he seemed to have a strange affinity.

Stuck in the country, frustrated, deprived of any outlets for her ambitions, Margaret Latimer would have left her husband had she not felt, perversely, that would give him too much pleasure. Instead, she determined to revenge herself by making him as miserable as she was; and she tried to implement her decision through ever-increasing nagging, bickering, back-biting, any and every sort of unpleasantness she could devise.

But he showed no sign of misery—or, indeed, of anything else.

And the more she tried to disturb him, the more composed he seemed to get. Until one night over dinner, she managed to push him too far and he rose from the table and came quietly to where she sat. And then hit her so hard that he knocked her out of her chair—and unconscious.

When she came to she found herself in bed—her body badly bruised. And used.

Not long later, she found that she was pregnant.

When she told her husband, his fierce desire for her not to have the child made her all the more determined to. As it grew within her she hated it—because it was a part of him and because of what it was doing to her body—but she clung to it, took every care not to miscarry again. Simply because he hoped she would. And she had won and the daughter was born. And because the child had been conceived in hate and bitterness, it seemed only right to her to christen it Felicity.

For the hell of it.

Margaret planned that once the girl was weaned, she would leave her husband, leave the child he hated with him. It was a beautiful plan. Like all the best plans it went savagely wrong. She grew ill. Tired, listless, with hardly the strength of will to get out of bed—and subject without warning to pains that seared her brain to unco-ordinated fragments of pulsing fire and left her vacant and limp and with little knowledge or remembrance of what had gone before the pain.

Margaret's sickness got no better. Dr. Latimer called in the best medical men in the land. They could find nothing wrong with his wife. The trouble, they all agreed, was psychosomatic, mentally induced by the patient herself. Psychiatrists were called to her bedside but their arrival seemed to bring on the pain and their visits were discontinued. And all the while, Dr. Latimer looked after his wife with the best of possible care. If her hatred for her husband had not been so deep-seated, in her pain-free moments she might have changed her mind about him, for to every appearance he was tending her with the devotion of a saint. But her hatred didn't soften.

In view of which, it was strange that the thought he could be poisoning her never crossed her somewhat enfeebled mind.

Nor did it cross her daughter's as she entered the room now on her mission of death.

"Oh. It's you," her mother said without enthusiasm.

"Hello, Mama." Felicity smiled, coming in and shutting the door.

Her mother was lying, as always, propped up in her old four-poster bed by the window. She looked at Felicity now and sighed and turned her head away and stared out. The view was pretty—over lawns and woods to distant hills. Felicity looked at her mother and thought how pretty she was too, with her dark hair growing long and splayed out romantically in carefully arranged disorder on the pillow round her pale drawn face—and deep, wounded eyes . . .

"Well—what do you want?" Her mother turned her head and looked at her.

"I just came to see how you were, Mummy."

"How I am! How do you think I am? I'm *ill*. And sick to death of it!"

"I'm sorry."

"Oh, God! She's 'sorry.' What do you think—?" She broke off suddenly, her face corrugating with pain. Felicity watched, fascinated, as her mother's body tightened, contracted, her knees jerking up towards her face, her fists clenching and beating in spasms on the bed-clothes. Her breath was short, harsh pants. This one's a real dilly, Felicity thought. She smiled. Her mother's attack was the most painful she'd ever seen.

"Does it hurt awfully?" she asked sweetly, coming nearer the bed. "Poor Mumsy!" She knew her mother couldn't hear her, couldn't reply, was aware of nothing but the pain. The woman's eyes were tight tight closed now and she was rocking across the bed in agony.

Felicity took the meat skewer from behind her back.

She looked at it, holding it up before her face, turning it and watching the afternoon light from the window glint along its spiralled edge. She prodded the point with a finger. It was nice and sharp. She walked closer to the bed. But some feet away, she could see that her mother was moving about far too much for her to get in a decent shot. She decided to wait till the attack passed and she'd have a static target. She pulled up a chair by the edge of the bed. And sat. And waited. After perhaps five minutes, as suddenly as it had begun, the tension went out of her mother's body; her breathing deepened and slowed; she lay, eyes closed, sweat-filmed, drained, back on the bed.

"*Now!*" the Voice screamed.

Felicity nodded quietly to it and got up from her chair. She held the skewer tight in her hand, let it hang by her side, walked slowly, controlling her excitement to the side of the bed. Her mother's face was not many inches below the level of her own. She examined it. It looked serene. She stared fixed at her mother's throat. She could see a vein in it pulsing ever so slightly.

She took aim, measuring the distance in her mind. Her hand tightened on the skewer.

Margaret Latimer opened her eyes.

Felicity's rising hand froze. Just below the bed and the level of her mother's vision. Her own pale eyes startled wide. She stared into her mother's lucid hostile gaze.

"What are you doing there?" Her mother's tone was sharp. She elbowed herself up in the bed to a sitting position. She was higher than Felicity now. "You just love to watch me suffer, don't you?"

"N-no, Mum—I—"

"Can't even talk, can you? Just like your father," her mother interrupted before she could fumble out more words, "a wax dummy. You belong in Madame Tussaud's!"

"Uh . . ."

"Run away and leave me in peace." Margaret Latimer stared coldly at her child and then deliberately turned her head away and looked out the window.

Felicity looked at the back of her mother's neck. There was sweat on it. It reminded her of the froth on a toadstool. Screening the meat skewer with her body, she turned and walked quietly out of the room.

She wasn't half-way down the corridor before the Voice was shrieking at her: "Cissy! Cissy! Can't do anything. Rotten little dummy."

"Shut up!" she screamed out loud at it, stopping dead in the passage.

"Weedy," it mumbled sulkily, and then was still.

"That's better," Felicity said—in her mind this time—and began to walk again. "I didn't have a chance to do it anyway."

"You *did.*"

"Oh sure," Felicity sneered, "when she was squirming like a chopped-up snake all over the bed. I just couldn't have missed, could I?"

"You could have done it after," the Voice said petulantly.

"There wasn't time."

"Was!"

"You think you're just so smart, don't you?" Felicity snapped back, starting to run down the stair. She leaned on the banisters. They gave.

"Watch it!" the Voice yelped.

Felicity jumped back; stayed close to the wall as she went down the stair. "Puh!" she went on. "Just suppose I had just managed to do it—not that there was the chance—what would have happened then? Huh? You tell me that!"

The Voice was silent.

"Well, I'll tell *you*. I'd have gone to jail—that's what. They'd have known it was me. I'd have been hanged most likely. A lot of good *that* would have done me!"

The Voice started to titter.

"Very funny. I *don't* think," Felicity sulked.

"Silly," the Voice said gently, "that was just a test—to see if you had the guts."

"Huh!"

"You've got to find a way so no one knows!"

"How'll I do that, huh?"

"Hah! Rat-tit-ti-tat, curiosity killed the cat—remember?" The Voice began to giggle and then its giggle got fainter and it was gone.

Felicity continued down to the bottom of the stairs. Angry and thinking hard. That was the clue all right. But she couldn't work it out. She went on to the nursery where she started to play: she mashed up some of the cockroaches that she kept in a box there, but the crunch of their backs under her penknife failed to provide its usual pleasure and turned out now to be just a bore. She was obsessed with unriddling the way to kill her mother. Before it had been just another game. Now it was a matter of honour. She thought about it all the rest of the afternoon. Come dinner, she had decided that maybe the way was poison.

From the earliest years she had been allowed to come and go as she pleased—to stay up all night if she wanted to. She usually took dinner in the nursery, but tonight she decided to have it with her father in the dining room. He was reading and seemed surprised and not pleased to see her but didn't say anything. Over dinner she tried to get a conversation going but he merely grunted and she found she was talking to herself. But when she asked him if there was any way to poison someone so no one else would know he looked up from his book.

"Why do you want to know that?" he asked, staring at her with a flat empty face.

"I just wondered. That's all."

He looked at her like he was examining her. Then suddenly almost smiled. "You have a strange mind for a little girl," he said—and looked back at his book.

"Daddy . . ." she went on, not wanting to let the matter drop.

"Be quiet and let me read in peace!"

"But . . ."

He looked up at her one final time from the book and she was sure there was a slight smile about his lips. "There is no indetectable way to poison anyone. None at all."

She was pretty certain he wasn't telling the truth, but she knew she wouldn't get anymore out of him and she ate the rest of her meal in sullen silence. If he wouldn't tell what poison to use, why she'd . . . she'd think of another way!

But dinner ended and she still hadn't.

She left the dining room, wandered into the hall; with no particular purpose, slowly began to climb the stair. After the second floor, she paused and sat on the steps. She sat there a long while. She saw the lights go down in the hall below her; heard the sounds of the dining room being cleared and later of her father going to bed. Time went on. But it left her outside it. A little girl in a private universe that was a stair. There were nooses and axes and guns and guillotines and bombs and acids in her mind. They scuttled back and forth after each other like sand crabs on a shore after low tide. They waved their claws at her.

"You'll get piles!" chirped the Voice.

"What?"

"Sitting on the floor gives you piles. It's a fact."

"Who says?"

"*I* do!"

86

"Huh! Fat lot you know."

"I know how to kill your mummy!" the Voice mocked in sweet tones.

Felicity got up. Began to climb. As fast as she could. "And so do I!" she gave back angrily.

"Bet you don't," goaded the Voice.

"Oh yeah? Well you just wait and see!" Felicity replied as she went on climbing. In fact she had no idea at all of what she would do. Her words were pure bravado. Until she came to the final landing. And then she had it. All at once everything was clear. She smirked to herself with satisfaction.

"Just you wait!" she repeated.

The landing was in darkness and Felicity made no attempt to turn on the light. Instead, keeping close to the wall and well away from the rickety banisters, she walked slowly through the darkness towards her mother's room. She moved as she had done earlier that day—but now with even greater care to be silent.

It took her nearly fifteen minutes to cover the twenty-five yards to her mother's bedroom. But in that time she had made no sound at all.

Now she stood outside the door. There was a crack of light coming from beneath it. Super! Had her mother been asleep, the plan couldn't have worked. As it was she would be either reading in bed or sitting in front of her dressing-table mirror in long and nostalgic self-contemplation. Either would do fine.

"Well? Go on then!" the Voice demanded loudly.

"Just you shut up—see?" Felicity hissed at it in her mind. "You don't be quiet and I won't do anything. Not now. Not ever!"

"All right, keep your hair on!" the Voice replied offendedly, and was still.

That's more like it, Felicity thought, angrily turning her attention back to what she had come to do. Her mother was in bed. She could hear the sound of its springs squeaking slightly as the woman altered position. Right! Felicity stretched out an arm and very softly, very rhythmically, began to scratch on the door. After a moment she paused to see if she had had any effect. She hadn't. As far as she could tell, her mother read on without hearing. Felicity tried again. A bit louder. But again without result. Felicity paused and pouted. Old Mummy must be going deaf. It wasn't fair. This would teach her! Felicity clenched her knuckles and rapped on the door.

Rat-tit-ti-tat.

She spaced out the taps as long as she could without losing the rhythm. And between each one she paused and listened. She didn't tap very loud. But she tapped loud enough. She could sense the sudden silence from behind her mother's door. It was almost as if the woman wasn't breathing in her efforts to listen.

"Who's there?" Margaret Latimer called out softly at last.

Felicity, of course, did not reply.

"Is anyone there?" Margaret demanded, more confident now.

Felicity waited. In silence. Waited till she heard her mother give a sigh that was half anger, half relief and settle back into her bed. Then she tapped once again. Soft and slow on the door. Again she could sense the unnatural stillness that followed her action. The room had gone quiet as a coffin. Then her mother spat out a short word that Felicity didn't understand and very noisily began to get out of bed and stomp towards the door of the room. Felicity took up her position.

Her mother opened the door.

The door was hinged to swing outwards from the bedroom into the end wall of the hall. It was a useful piece of design, for now as Felicity stood with her back pressed to the wall, she was hidden by the door. Through the crack between it and the jamb she could see her mother. She wore a dark velvet nightgown, was only inches from her on the threshold. She had paused there, was staring out hesitantly into the darkness of the passageway. Felicity wanted to giggle. Her mother looked so scared.

"Felicity?" she queried timidly.

Felicity felt her heart pounding. It seemed so loud and violent she was half-surprised her mother didn't hear.

"I know it's you," the woman continued uncertainly. She took a hesitant step out into the passageway: "Come on now!" She moved out along the passage in the beam of light from the door.

Her hand groped along a wall as she walked—searching a light-switch; but she'd obviously seldom come out in this passage at night, for she failed to find one.

Felicity listened. And waited. And when she judged that her mother had moved some way out into the corridor, she slowly and noiselessly came out from behind the door.

"Felicity?" her mother called with her back to the bedroom—at the furthest stretch of the light from the open door. Dimly beyond it, Felicity could see the outline of the balustrade. She began to walk—on tiptoe—towards her mother.

"This is no time of night to be playing silly games," the woman gave out to the dark corridor in general. As she was talking Felicity came up behind her. Margaret Latimer stood listening as her words died into the dark, then started to turn to go back to her room.

"Boo," Felicity said.

With a gasp of shock, Margaret Latimer jumped back. But not far enough for Felicity's liking. She hurled herself at her mother. And pushed. And though a seven-year-old weighs little and does not have much strength, neither do the legs of a woman who spends most of her time on her back in bed.

Felicity's mother tottered, lost her balance, scrabbled back—to the banister railings behind her. They were old and tired. Quite quietly and not very dramatically, they gave. And Margaret Latimer went after them.

She fell the four storeys without making a sound.

But her body hit the flag-stones with a sort of spread-out thump that carried right to the top of the stairs. Felicity moved cautiously towards the broken banisters and then, lying down on her tummy, crawled till she could peer over the edge. Her mother was a small shape down there. Like a soggy log squdged out on the floor. There was a little light and as her eyes adjusted to it and the distance, Felicity could see that her mother was on her back and her face was pointing up towards her and maybe it was some trick played on her sight by the distance, but it looked like the woman's eyes were open.

Felicity crawled back and stood.

"Wow!" the Voice said.

"Wow!" she agreed in her mind.

And then she and the Voice came together and were one. And perhaps because the game was over and it was the best there'd ever been, they both didn't know whether they wanted to giggle or cry.

CHAPTER 6

WHITE-EYED, black-haired, ten-year-old Felicity Latimer took her place on the railway seat between the young man and the woman. The brown-eyed handsome man and the woman. She felt a smug sense of belonging. Their black auras sandwiched her. She was a sliver of coal, gleaming and in its proper place, pressed around in blind earth.

Felicity looked at the woman reading the magazine on her right. In her mind she became a long and vertical bone. Cold and blooded near the top. She turned her head to stare at the man and found he was staring at her. He smiled at her with a "hello-little-girl" sort of smile. She hated it when people smiled at her like that. She opened her vast eyes to their full stretch and strobed them at him. It seemed to confuse him and he turned away towards the window. It was her turn to smile.

After a moment she gave her attention to examining the mountainous priest on the opposite seat. Peacefully reading his breviary, he was perhaps the most exciting of them all. Her mind transformed him: changed the robes on his back to gleaming sable starred with inverted pentagram and upside-down cross; stripped the prayer-book from his hands, replaced it with sacrificial dagger; saw him lift the knife over tiny man-thing squirming naked on an altar—and plunge down his hand. And the noises of the station merged into the fantasy and became the fevered cry of a hooded congregation exulting at the sacrifice.

It was a beautiful vision. She would love to see it with her real eyes—but then there was so much that real eyes could never see. It was sad. She closed them to try to hang on to the vision, but it was fading. Perhaps because she was uncomfortable. For she was sitting straight up with her back against the seat and her legs didn't even touch the floor. She slid herself forward till they did and then leant back again. This way she was pretty low down, much lower than anyone else, but she felt better.

Again she closed her eyes.

She started to concentrate on blackness. She made it flood on into her brain. If she could fill her mind with it, pictures would start to come, would swim in it like newts, and if she slid up on one and got to examine it before it got away, it would show her a glimpse of a different place and very often ahead into a different time.

For at the age of ten, Felicity Latimer was a princess and a priestess and a harlot and a mother and a crone, and she was witch of all the world.

But now as she opened her mind to clear-seeing, the pictures that came into it were not of the future. They were of the past. Of the night her mother fell . . .

She had made no move to go to the woman but had left her lying on the flag-stones and crept quietly down to bed. There, she had lain in the dark for a long time, too excited to sleep, straining her ears to the noises of the house at night and wondering how soon it would be before anyone came and found the body. When at last sleep came to her, she went to it with a sense of being compact and secure and come-together—perhaps because she knew that the Voice was within her and had gone deep into the inside of her and would never come out again.

The next morning, eagerness to find out what had happened woke her early and she had to force herself to stay in bed. Finally, when it was breakfast-time, she got up, dressed, and walked as casually as she could to the dining room. To get there, she had to cross the hall. It was just like normal and she tried to do it like she normally did. It was a huge effort. For she couldn't help expecting to trip across a corpse, even though her mother's body must have been taken away some time before.

She went in to breakfast. Her father was in his place as usual behind his newspaper.

"Morning, Daddy!" she said as always—and sat down. As she reached for the cereal, she noticed he was putting down his paper and looking at her. She focused all her attention on sprinkling her plate with corn flakes.

"Felicity!"

"Yes, Daddy?" she replied, looking up obediently and at once.

His face was blank. It always was. He stared her blankly in the eye for a long moment. Then he said: "I want you to prepare yourself for some very bad news."

"Yes, Daddy," she answered bravely.

"It's about Mummy."

"Yes."

"Your mother had a terrible . . . accident last night."

"Ac-accident?" The tremble in her voice was masterful.

"She fell from her landing into the hall."

"*Fell*—oh no! Is—is she—hurt?"

"Very."

"She's not . . . ?"

". . . dead?" he finished the sentence for her.

"Yes." She nodded numbly. Looked down at the tablecloth. Forced tears into her eyes—chortling inside her, as she did so, with admiration at her acting.

"No," he replied.

The word took a second to penetrate Felicity's awareness. When it did, all the acting skill in the world couldn't prevent her mouth dropping open with shock and her eyes flashing up to her father. For a second she just gaped at him. Dumbfounded. Feeling suddenly cheated. Too shocked to notice the strange half-smile that flickered beneath his expressionless face. Then she recovered and managed to mutter:

"She's all right?"

"She's alive."

"Oh! That's wonderful!" Felicity put all the enthusiasm she could into the words, but was disorientated once again when her father broke into a visible smile."

"It's not quite as wonderful as all that," he said. His smile died. "She broke her spinal column when she fell. She's totally paralysed."

"Para . . . ?" Felicity queried.

"Unable to move. Any part of her. At all."

"Then she can't—she can't—talk?"

"Talk? A fly could walk in and out of her mouth and she couldn't even twitch to shake it off!"

"How long will this para . . . thing last?"

"In all likelihood, your mother will be totally paralysed for the rest of her life."

Felicity sat dumbly trying to absorb the staggering news. She was saved from having to say anything more by her father abruptly rising.

"I'm going to her now," he said. "Come up when you've eaten breakfast. Doubtless, she'll want to see you." And he left.

Felicity sprinkled sugar on her corn flakes and began to eat. Unable to move for the rest of her life—she thought. How jolly. Of course it would be up to her to make sure that was not very long. She helped herself to more sugar.

Felicity had a sweet tooth.

But the taste in her mouth as she stood by her mother's bedside and looked down into her still and open eyes was mixed. There was sweetness all right in seeing her mother lying there with hate and fear bursting from her and yet being totally immobile and powerless. There was bitterness in the sense of personal failure that the woman was still alive. And there was a dull chalky taste that if she could have survived that fall, she might somehow survive this paralysis and come to take revenge.

Felicity stood beside her father and listened to him mumbling platitudes of love and reassurance and did her best to do the same—but she couldn't wait for him to leave the room, for more and more she imagined that at any minute her mother would suddenly open her mouth and say, "She pushed me!" But of course she couldn't and finally Felicity's father left and she went with him.

She came back again later. In the evening. Alone.

Her mother was lying exactly as she had been that morning. Were it not for the faint sound of her breathing, and slight tremor in the staring eyes as Felicity moved through their field of vision, there was nothing to show she wasn't dead. Felicity sat on the edge of the bed where her mother could see her.

"Hello, Mummy," she said softly with a little smile, "here I am again! Isn't that nice?" For just a moment Felicity was frightened her mother might reply or move or sit up and strike her—and then something about the woman's total immobility, her frozen stillness brought it home to Felicity that she could not, would never, move again.

"Can you hear me, Mumsy, darling? I 'spect you can. It would be such a shame if you couldn't, now wouldn't it? I mean you'd miss hearing what I'm going to do—to you! We wouldn't want that now, would we? No. Of course not!"

She got up, went to check there was no one at the door. Then she came back to the bed. For the second time in that room Felicity held a meat skewer. But now she displayed it with confidence, held it close to her mother's eyes.

"See that, Mummy? Do you know what it's for? Of course you do. It's for spiking into people's eyes with!" She darted the point at her mother's eyes—stopping it only a millimetre before contact. "Pretty close, wasn't it? Just imagine it—how that'll feel! You can't get away and spoil the game now like you did last night. You've already cheated once—and rotten cheats deserve to get spiked!" She held the skewer in her clenched fist and drew it back. Then she noticed that huge silent tears were seeping up from her mother's eyes.

"Cry-baby!" Felicity sneered. "Weedy, mouldy *wet!*" She was suddenly angry. "You're blubbing. That's all you can do—just blub!" Whereas before, she had been doing it to frighten her mother, now she desperately wanted to jab the skewer at her in earnest. With difficulty she restrained herself, realising that to do so would be to destroy herself as well. She untensed her arm, put down the metal. She got up from the bed and looked down at her mother with a face now coldly composed.

"Good night, Mummy," she said politely.

Then Felicity Latimer withdrew one of the pillows from behind her mother's back and held it over her face. She positioned it delicately, without any roughness. She pressed down gently. But sufficiently firmly to ensure that within a short space of time what minuscule movement there was about her paralysed mother became no movement. No movement at all.

Felicity removed the pillow. She put her ear to the open lips. Nothing. She stared into the open eyes. They looked the same. Except that something once in them you could only have sensed had been there was now gone.

Felicity lifted her mother's head. Put back the pillow behind it. She stood back from the bed and looked a little. The game is well and truly over now, she thought.

And feeling a bit blank about it all she turned and left the room.

With the death of Margaret Latimer, more than a game was over. For Felicity and Robert, her passing brought a new—and considerably poorer—life. Margaret had had funds. Not one penny of them went to her child or husband. Even the house had been assigned to someone else—a stranger.

For Robert Latimer, who had no money of his own and as a country doctor earned little, it was a blow. But he didn't seem to care much and he and Felicity left the big house and moved into a cottage in the village. And perhaps Robert Latimer did have something after all, for at least their maid, the one with un-healthy eyes and skin, moved in with them.

Six months after they'd settled in there, Felicity saw her first Reflection.

She was walking back from school. The school was a little way outside the village where they lived on the other side of a stretch of deserted pasture-land. A small river flowed through this down to the village and Felicity had paused on a bridge over it to throw stones at water rats. It was a pretty frustrating past-time because, even when there were any rats around, she didn't often hit them—and even when she did, they were seldom hurt. Now she waited, stone in hand over the river, and there was no motion other than the water, no sound other than its shallow, clear movement over stones, no presence other than her own. She gazed at her reflection. Black-haloed, it rippled along the water.

And then there was another reflection beside her own.

It shimmered. Gathered definition. It was a woman. Tall with long dark hair hanging long like her own. Felicity felt the warmth squeezed out of the sunshine. She was cocooned in cold. She didn't need to see any clearer to know who the woman beside her was.

"The rats have all gone," her mother said in a voice that tumbled and tinkled and laughed like the running water which reflected her.

Felicity turned her head then.

Margaret Latimer, the woman she killed, her mother six months dead and gone to dust in the grave, was standing by her side on the bridge. Felicity faced up at her. Her mother's face was bloodlessly pale. It had substance—there was a sense of skull behind the forehead—but it was fluid round the edges and it seemed to Felicity as if a powerful wind might suddenly blow through it from cheek to cheek and rub it away.

"Hello, Mummy," Felicity said, feeling cold from the Reflection but unafraid from somehow knowing that this mother had entered a different order of existence—a subordinate order—from which she could come with no power to harm her.

The Reflection of her mother laughed—a sound of anguish—and it lifted thin arms and fluttered fingers like reeds towards Felicity's throat. Instinctively, Felicity backed. She felt the bridge press against her spine—and understood in that moment what the presence was trying to do. She stood up straight towards it.

"I do that to *you,"* Felicity sneered.

The fingers went round her throat. But they were only cold fingers of wind. Searing stripes of coldness that faded on the warmth of the living flesh as the spirit in body faced out the spirit alone and sneered its hate at it and drove it back into the winds.

"You're nothing!" Felicity triumphed. And perhaps she was right. For suddenly there wasn't anything there. And she stood on the bridge alone. She heard a rustle then and looked down towards the water. The fattest rat she had ever seen was creeping from rushes almost directly under the bridge and moving into the water. She lifted the stone she found she still clutched tight in her hand. The rat got into the water and started to swim. It passed below the bridge. She threw down the stone with all her force. She hit the rat on its skull. It went under the water and didn't come up again.

And that was how Felicity saw her first Reflection—her mother. She never saw it again. And the second Reflection she saw she didn't realise was one at all.

Until it had gone.

It was standing near the edge of the school playground—a small blond woman watching the children play, with a rather sad expression on her face. Felicity felt the woman's eyes on her and looked at them and got the feeling as she did so that she was looking into tunnels that had no ending—but that was the only strange thing she noticed about the woman, who, she thought, was probably just someone's parent come to pick them up after school. Then the play period ended and the children drifted away, but Felicity noticed that the woman wasn't coming forward to claim any of them. She was just standing there wistfully.

And then she wasn't.

It wasn't much of an experience really. Except that Felicity realised somehow that she alone of all the children there had seen the Reflection and that it was aware that she alone saw it.

After that she began to see quite a lot of them. Maybe she had seen them before but hadn't known—but now she did. They weren't all the same. Some were very watery, just a sort of shiver down the wind which couldn't keep its shape and was very hard to see at all. Some were just like proper reflections seen flat in a mirror except that they were so flat that sometimes they weren't any thicker than a piece of paper, and sometimes they were so thin you could see what was on the other side of them. And there were some Reflections that you could never see properly at all but only guess at—shapes that moved in the corners of your eyes—but vanished when you turned your face to stare at them whole.

And then there were those Reflections which looked just as solid as people—and most were like this. At first Felicity would walk round them, and get out of their way when they came towards her just as if they were actually there. But then she learnt how to sense the difference between them and things of flesh—and then she used to just walk on straight through them. And that was a lot of fun. They hated it. It was a strange sensation walking through something that seemed solid but only left her with a feeling for a second like walking through the air from the door of an open fridge.

One summer evening she was on the common outside the village when an anaemic blond boy of about thirteen came up to her. She knew him immediately for what he was. She walked on ignoring him. By now, she was beginning to find Reflections a bore. She couldn't play with them; couldn't even hurt them. And they could do nothing to her. Or for her.

"Do you ever wonder where you are going?" the boy-form asked. Felicity looked round at it in surprise. Apart from her mother's, few Reflections had ever spoken to her before. For a moment she wondered if this wasn't a real person. He looked quite substantial walking there beside her and staring at her with a face which didn't look like it could ever smile. But then he didn't have the glow about him that people had and, like all Reflections, rather than pulse off force like people did he seemed to absorb it. And then Felicity looked at the ground and saw that his feet did not bend the grass.

"You talked!" she said to him, surprised.

"Of course."

"But you're just a—a Reflection."

"No. I am Substance."

They walked on together in silence while Felicity thought about that. But it didn't mean anything to her and she wasn't sure if she was really that interested anyway.

"Buzz off!" She told it.

"I can help you," it told her.

"Scram!"

"Really I can."

"Yeah? How?"

"I can give you things."

"Hah! Fat lot you can give me! You haven't even got a proper body to touch things with!"

"It's not that sort of thing."

"What sort is it then?"

"Would you like to see?"

"I don't mind."

"All right—sit down on the grass; cross your legs and your arms and stretch your right hand out on your left shoulder and your left hand out on your right."

Feeling slightly foolish, but curious to see what would happen, Felicity did as it asked. "Like this?" she asked.

"That's fine."

"It's soppy if you ask me!"

"I don't. Now close your eyes."

She did. Almost at once, was seized with an incredible sensation—wonderful and unlike anything she had ever known. She was lifted into darkness, soaring up into it. She was flying, sweeping wingless and weightless, swooping down avenues of night, down and down and wonderfully down.

"It's nice, isn't it?" he said—and her eyes were opened and

100

she was back on the ground sitting heavy there and feeling small and alone and feeble. She nodded to the boy-form.

"That's nothing to what I can give you," it said. "I can show you how to take yourself to different places while staying where you are. And I can teach you how to make people do what you want them to and how to hurt them without it ever showing or them knowing you have done it. And I can give you wonderful feelings and beautiful things in your mind."

Felicity believed it.

"What do you want from me in return?" she said practically.

"Your friendship. Forever."

Felicity didn't believe that. There must be a lot more to it than just friendship. There'd be a catch somewhere for sure. Still, it didn't do any harm right now to agree.

"All right." A pause, then: "Since we're to be friends, my name's . . ."

"Felicity." It finished for her.

"How do you know that?"

"I know everything."

Felicity didn't believe that for a moment either, but she didn't want to antagonise it just yet so she asked it sweetly: "Well, what's your name then?"

It didn't reply.

She looked at it then and it was huge and it wasn't a boy anymore. And it was no Reflection either. It smiled. Its smile was blood and snakes and sighs and burning and the death rattle of men.

Then Felicity knew who her new friend was and she knelt on the earth before Him.

The train gave a little jerk. It jerked her mind towards the present. Yes, the years had been good: He had kept his promise. Happy and at peace, she nestled back into the comforting evil she could still feel lapping around her.

For the first time in her life, Felicity Latimer felt a sense of coming home.

CHAPTER 7

Dr. Latimer looked across the compartment and saw his daughter smile to herself. Not for the first time, he reflected that the girl was insane. The thought no longer amused him. There had been a time when it had, when he first realised she had murdered her mother. It was ironic: he had been subtly, cleverly poisoning his wife over the years, methodically, carefully, with all the skill in the world; and then his daughter blundered along and, for no appreciable reason, effectively killed her in the most elementary way. Life was full, he thought, of such pointless little surprises.

For a time, thereafter, he derived a certain amusement from watching the progress of his daughter's lunacy. He found her recent phase, when she developed an avid interest in Satanism and was constantly addressing and worshipping things that palpably weren't there, the most rewarding of all. But now he was finally bored by the thing. When all was said and done, lunacy in the end became just as predictable and tedious as everything else in life.

And life was something Dr. Latimer no longer gave a damn for.

Deep down, for as long as he could remember, he had been bored. He realised he was probably born that way. Old. Without enthusiasm, without joy. There was a certain neat and packaged quality about it, he thought: being born all ready to die.

As his life progressed he found his interests encompassed almost nothing. Knowledge, power, all that wealth or beauty ever gave was nothing to him. By the time he had finished school and had to choose a career, he discovered he had only two even moderately sustained enthusiasms: a mild liking for sex and a slightly greater fascination in the process of degeneration—a joy, albeit moderate, in watching people fall apart. The first of these leanings involved him in marriage. The second made him a doctor— a position he used to study, and carefully and conspiciously assist in, the process of decay, whenever he possibly could.

The Hippocratic oath meant nothing to him. Dr. Latimer loved his fellow human beings almost exactly as much as he loved himself. And that was not at all. As a doctor, however, he found he could indulge all two of his interests almost at once—simply by using drugs to assist in the process of seduction. Addictive drugs which in their turn might in time lead to breakdown, suicide, or simply death. All could be interesting to watch.

And as far as he liked to do anything, watching was something Dr. Robert Latimer liked to do.

Or had.

Nowadays, there was really nothing left he liked. Even the spectacle of his own daughter's galloping homicidal lunacy no longer interested him at all.

So when two tickets for the Golden Arrow had come in the mail along with an invitation to attend a medical conference in Dover, Dr. Latimer had no wish or reason whatsoever to go. And none not to. He took Felicity with him, deciding that Dover

103

was as good a place as any to have her confined at last to an asylum.

Now, as he continued to look at her, still smiling into space, he realised that was quite definitely where she should go. And it wouldn't be long before they got there. For the time now was ten-thirty.

The train was moving out.

CHAPTER 8

THE pull-away was so gentle that, looking out of the window, Bill wasn't sure at first whether or not the train was moving. Then he felt a slight lurch and realised they were under way. Great! The start of a journey was always good news—especially this one. The Golden Arrow was shooting him off to a rich new life!

Slowly the platform began to slide past. Bill watched it with satisfaction. Staymore's eyes snicked up from his breviary, out the window, briefly at Bill, then went back to his prayer-book. Ann Cross didn't bother to look up from her magazine. Felicity Latimer stared straight in front of her at something no one else could see. And her father looking at nothing—so still and lifeless, he might as well have been dead.

So it was only natural that Bill alone should see the man.

Mackintosh slung, flapping, over his shoulder, he came running along the platform. Running hard. He drew level with their compartment, started to fumble with the door. But the train was accelerating and he could barely keep pace with it. Seeing this, Bill jumped up from his seat, flipped open the door and reached out an arm to him. He just managed to grasp it and Bill dragged him, almost lifting him off the ground, into the compartment. He pulled shut the door. The man stood panting. The train ran out of platform. It was moving quite fast now.

"Phew! Thanks!" the man gasped. He turned, threw his mac into the luggage rack, turned back to Bill. "Dead odd, you know —the other carriage doors were locked or something—blast 'em!" Suddenly noticing Staymore, he mumbled, "Oh—'scuse me." And sat down beside him.

"Thanks again!" he panted to Bill.

"Not at all," Bill replied, also sitting and glancing sideways as he did so at Ann Cross to see if the woman had noticed his gallant action. She hadn't.

"I must say it's the first time I've ever known a train to leave early!" the man went on.

Bill turned back to examine him. He was a scruffy-looking type. His tie was down his neck, his shirt open and dirty; his suit looked soiled—and he needed a shave. Bill suddenly felt less pleased at helping him into the train and he didn't bother to take in his words.

"Really?" he said dismissively, and looked out of the window.

"But it wasn't early. It left on time."

The voice was silvery clear and musical. The voice of a siren. Not a ten-year-old child. Everyone in the compartment turned and stared at Felicity. Everyone except her father. For he had heard that voice before—and besides, there was no music in his universe. Felicity let her disconcerting eyes move over the three men.

"It's just half-past ten," she said.

Over the top of the girl's head, Bill could see Ann Cross look towards him. Her face was expressionless. He looked at his watch. So did the newcomer.

"She's quite right!" Bill said to him civilly.

"Of course she is," the man replied, "that's the whole point, dammit—the train isn't meant to leave till ten-forty!"

Bill gave him a slightly superior smile: "'Fraid you got it wrong there, actually. Ten-thirty's the time."

The man looked at Bill, confused and a little angry, and then understanding began to come into his face. And with it a look of despair.

"This train does stop at Faversham, doesn't it?"

"Nope. It's non-stop all the way."

"All the way to where?"

"Dover of course."

"Dover!"

"That's right."

"Oh God!" The man was dejected. "I'm on the wrong train."

The scruffy man's dismay was comic. Felicity started to giggle. Bill felt himself beginning to laugh as well. He turned his head away in an effort to get himself under control. Even the priest, who was ostensibly reading his breviary, started to chuckle quietly—his huge body vibrating and rippling with amusement.

Ann Cross had overheard the exchange and now mentally snorted. Twerp, she thought, the train had "Golden Arrow" written on every coach. Perhaps he couldn't read. She almost felt like chortling as the two men and the little girl were. Realising that, she ceased to find the shabby man funny. It was odd, she thought, that she should feel the same way as these others. It gave her a sense of what was almost kinship towards them. She didn't like that.

"Oh Christ!" the scruffy man moaned.

"He won't help you now, I'm afraid," Bill couldn't help chuckling. And Felicity twittered at that.

"What am I going to do?" the man muttered to no one in particular, ignoring Bill and thinking out loud.

Staymore gave up any pretence of reading his breviary then and looked down at the man by his side. "You have two options," he said amicably, "the one is to pull that device above the door and stop the train. As the sign above it says, that shall cost you

£25. You will still have to walk back to the station. Your other option is to contain yourself until we reach our destination, then take a train back. I recommend you do that."

The man shifted, uncomfortable and embarrassed, under Staymore's address: "Thank you. Yes, of course. I'm sorry," he apologised. "I didn't mean to bore you and everyone with my problems." He smiled awkwardly to the rest of the compartment.

But suddenly no one was smiling at him.

The young man who had helped him into the train had started to read a newspaper. The little girl beside him had a look on her face so void she could have been made of wax. Beside her the elegant-looking woman was engrossed in a magazine. By the window next to him the rather obese priest was praying from a small black book. And on the other side of him the bald little man looked into the corridor.

The scruffy man sat back and stared unhappily out of the window. The train was going faster now. Taking him faster from where he wanted to be. It had slipped the station, let its long straggle behind, was rumbling through the grimed and dreary outreaches of unending city. House after identical house. Like an army of multi-storeyed tanks that had come to the side of a mighty river and had stopped their engines by the water—and atrophied. Houses where houses should never have been. Each butting its blank brick walls, long past grimed black with coal smoke, up to the railway tracks. Each offering to the diesel fumes its washing lines of smalls and nappies, which trembled as the houses themselves trembled as the trains went by. Gosh, the scruffy man thought, people shouldn't have to live in places like that. He was suddenly thankful for his own nice little suburban house, his wife and clean kids. And he wished like the blazes he were going home to them now!

Clackety-clack.

A metallic sound from beneath them.

Their carriage crossing points, perhaps. Certainly not an unusual noise to hear on a train. Indeed, of the six people in the compartment, Felicity Latimer alone was consciously aware of it. But hearing it sent a gush of ice down her spine. For what she heard was not the friendly sound of train wheels on train tracks. It was quiet, impersonal, final. The first moving part of a gigantic trap which piece by inexorable piece was starting to close around the train—and all of them in it. And though the realisation of what that sound was and what it meant for them excited her and set her senses tingling, she was surprised that somehow it didn't make her feel good at all.

If Felicity felt strange, however, the scruffy man opposite her felt more and more like death all the time.

His wife had been right—blast it! She almost always was. But, he still didn't see why he shouldn't have gone. After all, stag parties weren't an everyday occurrence and neither was the engagement of the friend this one had been given for. But of course she didn't see it that way at all. To her it was just another feeble excuse for a lot of childish, downright retarded, men to go and get beastly drunk. And she had pretty dark suspicions about what they went and did after that. Of course, that part wasn't true, but he had to admit they did have a drink or two. Lord, did they! He'd missed the last train back the night before; he'd been too ill to show up at the office this morning; now, trying to crawl back home, he was still so fuzzed he'd gone and caught the wrong train. There wasn't a chance in a million she'd ever believe it. No. She'd skin him alive.

Ow!

As if the thought of what his wife had waiting for him wasn't enough, a whole polo team on bicycles was starting to pedal furiously up along his spine into the back of his skull. There, they were taking random swipes with their sticks at what was left of his brain. Oh gawd. He needed a drink. Ugh—no! He'd never touch the stuff again. Hey! Maybe he could get some sleep. Not a chance. Hangovers like this hurt too much to let you.

He closed his eyes.

Five minutes later, the scruffy man was snoring. Deeply, disjointedly. Between the doctor and the priest.

Ann Cross looked up at him coldly from her magazine. Noisy lout, she thought, what's he doing here anyway? Probably doesn't

109

even have a first-class ticket. Not that travelling first-class was much guarantee of the class of one's company. She swept her glance along the opposite seat and then looked out into the corridor. The priest smelt. The scruffy man snored. The man beside him stared—had been gorping at her for some time now. God, what a collection! There was a time trains used to be glamorous. Now they'd gone all to pieces. She'd have done a lot better to have taken the plane after all. Well, she'd know for the next time.

If there was a next time.

The thought came unprompted into her mind and for no reason. Like a little voice from a dark room that when the lights are turned on is shown to hold no one at all. It startled her. Then it made her angry. That was sloppy, weak thinking. Why shouldn't there be a next time? If she wanted one, there was damn well going to be. No question about it. She ceased to look out at the rather dismal empty corridor and turned her head to face the man opposite. He was still staring at her. Still! God, he must have been ogling her non-stop since the moment the train pulled out. Ann grew more angry. Who did he think she was? Some pin-up for him to drool at all the way to Dover?

She stared back cold into his eyes.

What happened then surprised her. He did not look away. Did not seem to notice she was glaring at him. He just went on studying her with the objective detachment of an art critic examining a portrait that is beautiful—but flawed. It wasn't how she'd expected him to look at all. She'd anticipated meeting a furtive little glance that would crumble the moment she confronted it. Instead, he was just staring relentlessly back at her with the immobile, bland, expressionless face of a snake—and with eyes that had as much depth and emotion as two chips of reflective tin. Ann had never been looked at this way before. It was a staring-match she clearly could not win. Dammit! Ann Cross lost out to no man.

"Having fun?"

She addressed him with the easy put-down of a woman of the world accustomed to flicking off nasty little men as casually as a horse flicks off flies with its tail.

110

His face remained expressionless, but his pupils clicked like twin camera shutters. "I beg your pardon?" he replied.

"Do you just?" Ann permitted herself a slight sneer.

"Sorry?"

Ann talked down to him. Wearily. A lady forced to communicate with a peasant in every way her inferior. She said: "Did no one ever tell you—it's rude to stare?"

"Oh! Oh dear. Have I been staring at you? How very thoughtless of me. I *do* apologise."

His voice as he said this was without inflection, his face expressionlessly flat. Ann could not tell if he meant what he said or was trying to provoke her, but were it calculated to annoy her, his reply could not have been more successful. When she spoke back to him she wasn't so poised.

"Try the window," she suggested. "That's what it's there for."

"But of course," he replied smoothly with a smile so flat it didn't part his lips. And dismissively, calmly, he turned away and looked out.

Ann seethed. She had got the worst of the encounter and she knew it. What made it more annoying, the cocky young man had been listening. She felt him watching her now, amused and conscious as she was that she had made a fool of herself. For a second she considered an apology to save face. No! She'd be damned if she would. What did it matter what this bunch thought anyway? None of them could ever be any use to her. She resumed her magazine. At least the man had finally stopped gorping, so she'd achieved what she set out to do, after all. She slid a glance up from the magazine. Oblivious of the snoring man by his side, he was staring towards the window in much the same way as he had stared at her. Man's most likely mental, she thought. As she did so, something made her look to her left. The little girl who sat beside her was smiling up at her. Now she nodded and winked—almost as if she knew Ann's thought. And agreed.

Ann stared at the child a moment, confused. And, for some reason she couldn't pinpoint, a little worried. It was odd, that. The child . . . the whole journey so far . . . odd. She felt there was something about it all that was—she wasn't sure what— unnatural. Not right. She shook herself mentally. This sort of pointless worrying wasn't like her at all. And anyhow, when you came to think of it, what could go wrong on a train?

Ann Cross dismissed her feeling of unease, determinedly directed her attention back to her magazine.

As she did so, the Reverend Sullivan Staymore shut his breviary. He laid his heavy palm upon it a moment in a sort of benediction, then he placed it in a pocket of his long black robe. He hadn't missed a word of the woman's vicious attack on the perfectly harmless gentleman who sat just a place away—and neither, he noticed, had the nice young man opposite. Staymore saw him regarding the creature with a look of disapproval—a sentiment he entirely shared. Now the young man was looking at him. What gentle brown eyes! The darting sensitive eyes of a fawn. As they caught his for a second, it was clear to Staymore that the two of them thought exactly alike. Indeed, without a word being spoken, he felt they had conversed. "Aren't women wretched?" the young man had conveyed to him. And he had responded: "Yes. Indeed they are!"

It struck him that a nice male bond had been forged between them.

"A lovely day," Staymore said.

"Yes, it is," Bill agreed, rather blankly, looking out.

"A peaceful day," Staymore went on.

"Yeah."

"It is days like this that fill one with a sense of goodwill."

"Umm."

What on earth was the priest babbling on about? Bill wondered. His remarks had seemed sort of arch. As if there were some meaning in them other than the obvious one. He couldn't be having a dig at the woman for her very obvious lack of goodwill towards the old boy opposite, could he? Yes, why not? And if he were, that was something Bill wanted to get in on.

"Yes, indeed," Bill said gravely. "It's a shame there can't be more peace in the world."

"Ah yes!" Staymore quickly rejoined, "and there would be—if only we could learn to *love* one another."

Hah! Not bad! Bill thought, turning to grin at the priest. But the vast man's deep-eyed smile as he looked back at him gave the words a suddenly fuller meaning and Bill looked away. Good God, he thought, the vicar's a queer. It's impossible. Shocking. Surely he couldn't be. Bill glanced at Staymore again. He was still smiling towards him in a revoltingly comradely way. Bill made a polite smirk somewhere towards the gleam of the man's thick spectacles—and to his dismay saw a responding quiver in the blubbery lips in face of him that confirmed his doubts. Hell, Bill thought, what a sick world where even the clergy are bent. He looked out the window, somehow saddened, in disgust.

Funny thing—it really was quite a nice day.

It struck the Reverend Sullivan Staymore that way also. And gazing out at it, he felt emotionally replete. The young man had responded well; had instantly realised the reprimand intended; had assisted him in delivering it, but had shown, as he himself had also, an admirable restraint. Staymore only hoped the wretched woman had heard and understood. In his secluded years as headmaster, he had come into contact with so very few women, he had almost forgotten how despicable they were. But still—it was hard to have stern thoughts just now. For, as the train moved thrustfully through the countryside, it seemed that God himself was smiling down on it. Such a blessed, beatific day! It was even on a day like this, no doubt, that the Lord must have led his chosen into the Promised Land.

The sky was cloudless. Gentle blue. Serene. The sun already high and warm over fields of early fall with the leaves going dry but still on the trees and the grass a deep rich green that tinkled fresh with the glisten of recent rain. The clean scent of cut meadowland wafted through the window into the compartment.

It was the sort of day, Dr. Robert Latimer noted dryly, that was supposed to make a man feel glad to be alive.

He didn't.

Seldom had. In a vague sort of way he began to wonder if the tough, attractive woman opposite did either. Perhaps she too took little joy in life. But then perhaps she had, as they say, a ball. Either way, the proposition already bored him. As did the woman. As did this train. As did—

He noticed something.

For some time he'd been staring at it without realising there was anything noteworthy about it. Now, suddenly, the strangeness of the normal sight he was seeing snapped into his mind and, doing so, struck him as so unusual it sparked a flicker of interest inside him.

It was a road.

Running at perhaps forty-five degrees to the direction of the train. A wide road by British standards. With enough room to hold—maybe four lanes of cars. But that wasn't very easy to estimate. Simply because there weren't any cars on the road.

Dr. Latimer looked at his wrist-watch. It had stopped at half-past ten. He sighed. It was little things like that which helped make life so exceptionally borish. Still—it was not important. He estimated they had been travelling for at least fifteen minutes. That would make the time a quarter to eleven. They could not have gone more than twenty miles outside of London. That near the metropolis at this time of day, it was inconceivable that a road this size should be without a single car.

And yet it was.

It angled with mathematical straightness away from the train. He could see along it for some miles. Nowhere was there a vehicle of any sort at all.

He sat back and thought. Perhaps the road was closed for repairs. But if so, where were the repair-men? No, that couldn't be it. And yet there had to be an explanation. He thought on, gazing dreamily in front of him, without reaching any conclusion and, when he looked out, the road was almost out of sight. It was at this point that he remembered there was something else about it that had lodged in his mind. What was it now? Ah yes—in patches he thought he had seen grass or weeds growing up through the tarmac. No. His memory must be playing silly

114

games, he decided. It was quite impossible for any highway in Britain that near a city ever to go to seed.

About as impossible as it being empty?

He nearly smiled. The whole thing was almost intriguing. It was one of the very rare incidents in life that raised questions he couldn't answer. Though for that matter, he thought, just as his mind slid once more into boredom, it was certain no one else here could either.

He was wrong.

Felicity Latimer had seen the road; had seen it was not a road like another; had known without thinking what that meant. And if someone had asked her to explain it, she could have—though maybe not in their terms. But as it was, no one asked for an explanation and she hadn't volunteered her knowledge. Even if she had, it wouldn't have helped. For all of them the information would have come at least fifteen minutes too late.

Clackety-clack.

The sound shivered her right along her body. She didn't know if it was excitement or fear. The second tooth on the trap snapping shut! Surely not so soon? Sure! The train was moving much faster—rattling along now, chuckety-chuck, chuckety-chuck, with the carriage swaying enough from side to side to make her have to sit up straighter in her seat, or risk being vibrated right off it. She duly adjusted her positioning. Doing so, she noticed the sleeping man opposite. He looked like a doll with the spine sucked out. He was wobbling from side to side with the movement of the train and it seemed it would only be a matter of time before he flumped down on either her father's shoulder or that of the priest. That would be fun to see, Felicity thought. She didn't reckon either man would play pillow to him very long.

Then she frowned.

What, she wondered, was the scruffy man really doing here anyhow? She knew how he got here, but he didn't fit in at all. The sort of light that flickered out from him was just the same old colour as that around most dull normal people. Just a dreary pale grey with splotches of bright in it and splotches of dark. It lacked the dense coal-blackness of the auras of the others. It was

115

out of place. Weedy. A tadpole in a pond of pike. He clearly didn't belong, was not meant to be here. And then Felicity thought about that and what it meant and she ceased to frown and found it very funny indeed.

CHAPTER 9

ANN Cross was restless.

The journal she was trying to read wasn't helping. Even though it was some minutes since the clergyman and that young character had stopped their puerile efforts to mock her, even though no one in the compartment now spoke, she found it impossible to concentrate. The words before her swam; meant nothing in her mind. The latest market quotations were a meaningless string of figures. She felt an ill-defined aggression towards her fellow passengers—and because she always tried not to feel any needless emotion or, feeling it, tried not to let it dominate her in any way, she was angry with herself. She looked through the window on her right out into the corridor. And through its windows in turn she watched the countryside rolling by—noting without much interest that it was really a lovely day for the time of the year. More like a day in late spring than autumn.

She looked in along the corridor. It was empty. Lifeless. And no one came past as she stared at it. But a little further, opposite the next compartment, she could see reflected in the corridor window the shapes of people inside the compartment. They were vague and nebulous. Skeletal mirror shapes that flickered and faded against the passing scenery like memories flickering over the mind before sleep. They had a disembodied quality and yet Ann found them somehow comforting—a reassurance. Against what she didn't know.

And then through her glass and that of the corridor outside it she saw a shape in a field. It was too far away for her to know what it was, but something about it compelled her attention. It was black. Seemed to float in the distance, fluid against the horizon. She strained her eyes towards it. And the progress of the train brought it nearer, nearer. She could see it better now. It was at the top of a stark and withered tree on a single skeletal branch that spiked up lewdly into the sun-filled sky.

It was only a bird.

As she realised that, Ann felt relief and disappointment. Relief because the shape had not only mesmerised her, it had somehow oppressed her; disappointment because the emotion had been engendered by something so everyday. But then she realised that was exactly what it wasn't. The train had got as close to it as it was going to and was now taking her away; Ann hadn't seen it clearly. She had neither interest in, nor knowledge of, birds—but she was suddenly convinced that this was no ordinary specimen.

It was big.

She couldn't judge how big, but it certainly seemed larger than she'd have imagined a bird could be. Much bigger than an eagle. And it was very black. Not black with the sheen of a crow—but with a dull darkness that struck no sparkle, seemed to absorb the sunlight. And even at its closest point, the bird had seemed oddly undefined. More than anything, it reminded Ann of a vulture; hump-backed, hooded, drooling. Like an old-

118

fashioned frock-coated undertaker standing peering into a grave —and cloaked in black against the sun.

It was gone.

Slid past with the land outside the train. Ann could have got up and gone into the corridor and walked down and maybe still got a view of it. But she wasn't really that interested. The creature had probably just escaped from a nearby zoo. And though it had looked macabre and discordant in the sunny day and green fields, it was gone now.

And, after all, it was only a bird.

She looked in at the corridor. It was still empty. And some change in the moving landscape must have altered the reflective quality of the windows—for the next-door compartment they mirrored now seemed to hold no one at all.

Ann shrugged and looked in once more at her own compartment. Only to see that the little girl beside her had picked up and was reading her fashion magazine. What a cheek! For a moment she was angry and felt an urge to snatch it out of the girl's hands. But she didn't. For she remembered that when she was young she wouldn't have asked to borrow the magazine either and she felt a sympathy for this child. She was only showing sense. People who asked in life didn't get. Those who took did.

"How do you like the new length?" Ann asked her dryly.

"Not bad," Felicity looked up to her. "You don't mind, do you?" she asked, gesturing with the magazine.

"Why should I?"

Felicity nodded and started to read again. After a while, her eyes on the magazine, she asked: "What's your favourite colour?"

"It depends. I'm not sure I've got one. I like—"

"I like black best," Felicity interrupted.

"Really? You're wearing blue."

"That's just a pretence."

"Ah!"

"A disguise."

"Oh yes?"

"You shouldn't ever let people see what you are," Felicity advised Ann seriously.

Ann couldn't help smiling at that. "Is that a fact?" she said.

Felicity looked up from the fashion magazine then and studied Ann. Ann kept her face expressionless as she looked back down at her. But the child's vast milky eyes were disconcerting. They were enveloping and hypnotic and faintly somehow horrible. They reminded Ann of a thing she had never seen: a frothing eruption of maggots hissing from the eye-sockets of a skull.

Felicity held out the magazine. "You have it back."

"Thank you."

"We won't be wearing these where we're going," Felicity suddenly smiled.

"No? And where . . . ?"

"Dover."

It was the balding man opposite who spoke. Ann looked across at him, a little surprised. Then he was talking on:

"My daughter and I are going there to attend a medical conference." A pause. He looked at Ann. "I'm a doctor, you see."

"Oh." Ann looked back at him—for some reason disconcerted and at a loss for anything to say. Polite as he now was, obviously harmless, there was something about this man she found a threat.

Dr. Latimer made a deprecating gesture. "I'm afraid you'll have to put down my rudeness in examining you to an occupational trait."

"That's all right," Ann replied, taking the words as an apology because she couldn't see what else they were and anyhow she was too busy trying to locate the source of her unease. What was it about this balding middle-aged man?

"Rather like housemaid's knee, you might say!" he went on.

And then she had it—the doctor reminded her of her father. God, what a revolting thought. He hadn't fumbled his way into her mind for years. And yet, there this balding little man was—in some quite definite but hard to analyse way his very reincarnation. Ugh!

"A disease I see you're not suffering from," he went on, look-

120

ing at Ann's legs. She looked down at them herself then, not following what he had said. "What?" she asked.

"Housemaid's knee," he repeated.

"Oh yes," Ann replied, "I didn't think anyone ever had that."

"No," Dr. Latimer replied dryly and took out a crumpled packet of untipped cigarettes and, without offering them to Ann, lit one—and then turned away.

Some doctor, Ann thought. Smoking and talking about housemaid's knee. The disease went out before the Boer War. She was glad she wasn't one of his patients. His hands looked more like those of a butcher than a surgeon. They weren't at all unlike her father's hands.

The thought made her shudder. God, she was beginning to have enough of this journey. She'd be glad when it was over. And that shouldn't be too very long now. She looked at her watch. Damn it! She'd recently paid good money for it—and yet the thing seemed to have stopped.

The only time it gave her was half-past ten.

CHAPTER 10

AND now it wasn't such a lovely day.

The train was speeding through deep country. Deserted. With grass grown long and brambled in thick fields by the railroad tracks. There was a wind. It blew along with the wind from the rush of the train, bent back the tall grass that grew so close to the train tracks, caught up thin clouds and whipped them across a greying sky and massed them and densed them into fuller clouds. And surrounded the sun. The sun ran from the clouds. Outran them, ran through them. But they packed towards it and chased it with the relentlessness of the sea and finally they closed in on it and got around and over it.

And the clouds smothered the sun and it did not come out again.

The Reverend Sullivan Staymore watched. Watched the death

of the sun. He found it fine. As indeed he did all aspects of the final thing. For wasn't that what religion was all about? Indeed! As a priest he had often stood by people's bedsides and, silently rejoicing, had seen their souls scuttle forth to meet the Maker. But this now—this destruction of the mighty sun—had a pomp and splendour, a ritual, almost sacrificial, quality about it that to his eyes was especially moving. Such must have been the deaths of the early martyrs in the Roman arena: battling, battling till in the end they were torn down and overcome by packs of wild beasts. Splendid! Those were the days, he thought. When faith was the gift of God and so strongly felt that a man would gratefully die for it—not like this wretched age when the Lord's good grace had to be beaten into parasitic wretches at the end of a cane.

He looked away from the window, his pin eyes spiking at the passengers on the facing seat.

The woman he had so justly mocked had somehow contrived to let her skirt ride up above her knee—exposing some of her thigh. Jezebel! Like all of her kind. Well, he would not cast the first stone, but he knew in smug certainty that the Lord had a place for those like her. Staymore looked to see who her flesh was being displayed for. Could it be the doctor she had so recently abused? Could it be the young man? Heaven forbid! Could it even be himself? It was impossible to say. And yet, why not? The depravity of woman knew no respect for the cloth.

He took out a handkerchief and wiped some sweat from his chins.

Then he moved his attention to the girl by the woman's side. He hadn't really studied her before and, doing so now, was struck despite himself. Much as he abominated her sex, Staymore was forced to admit that this was a veritable Madonna of a child. Her face, her extraordinary eyes, radiated innocence. There was no denying it. She had the countenance of a saint. It turned respectfully towards him.

"Hello," Felicity Latimer said.

"Ah!" Staymore replied after a second's pause.

"Can—can we talk?"

"Of course, my dear."

"There's some questions I'd like to know the answers to and I thought maybe you . . ."

"By all means!"

Staymore was delighted. It seemed the child wished to receive instruction in the Faith. Who knows? Perhaps if there were time he might even convert her! He glanced at his watch. Half-ten. The train didn't get in till nearly twelve. Perhaps that would be time enough. It would be a miracle—but what a story with which to edify the bishops when he got to Rome!

"You're a vicar, aren't you?"

"I am a priest."

"A *what?*"

"A Roman Catholic priest."

"Is that the same as a vicar?"

Staymore could sense the ears of the compartment tuned in on the conversation now. He decided to simplify. Straight-faced, without false modesty, he said: "It's better." No one contradicted him.

"Then you'd know, wouldn't you?" Felicity asked.

"Know what?"

"If it's true that if someone is very bad they go to hell when they die!" She leaned forward a little in her seat. She was eager.

Staymore was slightly taken aback. But, nonetheless, he admired the child's straightforwardness. She had come immediately to a major issue, a vital point of dogma. There was nothing to be gained by prevaricating.

"If they're very evil," he told her seriously, "and they do not repent their sins, yes—they go to hell."

"That's when they die?"

"Yes. Of course."

"But what happens if they *don't* die?"

Staymore smiled. "Everyone dies," he said.

"But just *supposing*," she persisted, "can you go to hell without dying?"

Staymore scowled. The words "of course not" were on his lips

124

—but they gagged there, unspoken. He realised suddenly that it was a tricky question. And—he wasn't sure of the answer. In all his years as a man of God, he'd never thought about that particular problem before and the solution was far from obvious. Jesus had risen in body from the dead and both he and the Virgin Mary had physically ascended alive into heaven. The resurrection of the body and everlasting corporeal life was an article of faith. But if the body went to heaven, it must also, quite clearly, go to hell. And if it could go living to paradise, then why not also to damnation?

"Well?" Felicity cut in on his quandary.

"No," he said firmly. "Of course you can't go to hell without dying!"

He wasn't sure why he said that—except that anything else was somehow unacceptable. He'd no sooner spoken than she smiled at him broadly. In a way he didn't like. He began to wonder if her question was serious anyhow—or just part of some silly and irreverent little joke.

"Thank you," she said, still smiling.

Staymore nodded. He did not return her smile. He was about to look away when she spoke again.

"Where are *you* going, then?" she asked.

Why to paradise, of course! Staymore thought, outraged—then realised that she couldn't conceivably have the impertinence to mean the question that way. "Most immediately to Rome," he told her frostily.

Again that infuriating smile. So witless. So serene. He began to revise his opinion of this child. Perhaps she wasn't innocent —merely stupid. Sourly, he realised he was unlikely to make a convert here. Hers was another soul that was outside his power to save and must go to Satan's legions. Ah well . . . such was the Will of the Lord.

At which moment, it became the Will of the Lord that the head of the scruffy man by his side should suddenly descend onto Staymore's mammoth shoulder like a boulder plopping into swamp. The priest quivered with surprise. Then, slowly and with dignity, turned his face to examine the man who now sprawled heavily against him—blissfully asleep. And snoring still.

"He's asleep!" Felicity trilled.

Staymore swivelled his eyes back at her. "So it would appear," he said.

"You're not going to wake him, are you?"

Staymore scowled at the brat. But before he could think of a suitable reply, the doctor spoke. He was facing the child, his expression curiously devoid of even acquaintanceship. He did not look at the priest.

"My daughter is curious," he announced.

Staymore wasn't sure in which sense of the word the doctor meant it and the man said nothing more. Either way, though, he quite agreed. The girl, however, ignored her father and as if he had not spoken went on intensely:

"You mustn't wake him up!"

Staymore decided that the best way to handle this impertinent child would be to ignore her. He did—turning his attention to the scruffy man slumbering against him. For a moment, he felt an almost maternal instinct towards him and thought of leaving him there to sleep. But he realised that wouldn't make a very dignified picture. And then he smelt alcohol on the man's breath —and that sealed it. No drunk was going to rest his besotted body against an Anointed of the Lord. No. He would deal with him now. Without delay.

Clackety-clack.

The Reverend Sullivan Staymore was thwarted. Even as he reached a huge hand towards the man, the train shook; their carriage swayed; he was conscious of the child sucking in her breath, as if in shock, and giving a little nervous giggle; and then the man shuddered away from his shoulder. Lolling upright on his own, without support, once more. And there he stayed. Looking boneless. A scarecrow that had somehow found its way onto a train. Reluctantly, Staymore let his hand drop to his lap. The man slept on without touching him—depriving him of any excuse to act. Wretch! Staymore thought. Spineless wretch. What he needed was a flogging! That'd put some backbone into him.

But alas, Staymore realised, he was not at school now. Such joys—or rather *duties*—would have to wait. Why had he thought joys, he wondered. That wasn't the way he felt about doing what the Lord required of him. No. He mustn't let the hypnotic movement of the train go and mesmerize him into thinking silly things like that!

Briskly he looked towards the window. Doing so, his glance swept over the young man opposite. There, at least, was a pleasant contrast to the drunk by his side. Neat, composed, correct—it was a pity there weren't more people like that. The wretched world would be a healthier, less sinful place.

His little eyes went out to the wide view outside.

Perhaps it was his imagination but it seemed to have got a lot darker. There was certainly no sign of sun and the clouds now were one unbroken plane of grey. Dark grey. Dense. Smoothly dispersed across the sky. Staymore found it a bizarre sort of sky and hard to predict whether or not it would rain. Though one thing was certain—below its slate greyness the country was wild. Surprisingly wild. In fact, nowhere could he even see a house. He was a little startled when he realised that. He hadn't thought that anywhere in England was there countryside so forsaken. Or for that matter so dismal. It had a rank, grown-over look about it as if it had long since ceased to feel the presence of man. Perhaps it was just the funereal day. It looked more like evening now than mid-morning. What was the time? Oh yes, he'd just looked. Ten-thirty. It really shouldn't be so awfully dim at this time of day . . .

The train went through the station.

It happened without warning. One moment Staymore was looking out at a vista of country, the next he had jerked back from a jumble of buildings hurtling close by his face. They must have been moving very fast indeed. For he had time merely to register a void and dusty platform and station empty of life and then all were gone and he was staring once more at desolate fields. The effect was disturbing. It was as if a projectionist had muddled the reels of a movie. In a leisurely, detailed longshot, had suddenly cut in a fast confused closeup—a closeup that had

127

no relevance to anything in the film that had come before or would again—then, realising his mistake, had cut out again at the precise point where he'd started. Country—station—country. The station had not belonged. Staymore was puzzled. He hadn't been on a train for some years and couldn't remember if going through a station was always like that. But he felt not. In some way that he couldn't precisely call to mind, he was sure it was different.

"Excuse me," he turned and asked Bill Armstrong, "but you didn't see the name of that station, did you?"

Bill looked away from the glass. His face, Staymore noted, was slightly puzzled—perhaps even annoyed. "'Fraid not," he replied. "We were going too fast."

"It didn't have one," Felicity Latimer said.

Bill looked round and smiled at her. "Really?"

"I think you'll find," Staymore said, "that all stations have names."

"No," Felicity replied determinedly. "Not *all* stations do."

Staymore was suddenly angry. "No? No?" he hissed, "well then perhaps you'd care to tell me one that hasn't!"

"That one we just passed," she replied pertly.

Staymore had trouble controlling his anger. The blood was in his face and his cheeks and chins were trembling—and not with the motion of the train. He was about to voice a reply. But from the opposite corner of the compartment, Ann Cross spoke first.

"She's quite right, you know. The station didn't have a name."

Staymore faced her. The light from the window played along his spectacles and his eyes behind them were narrowed and hard to see in the sweating fat of his face. "This is a silly discussion," he said, spacing out each word from the next and speaking slowly and very quietly. "You will appreciate that each and every railway station is both a point of departure and of *arrival*. As such, it has to be recognisable—which it could not be without a name. No one would know whether or not to get off at it. As a station it could not function—could not exist!"

"I'm sure you're quite right . . ." Ann Cross said gently.

"Of course I am!"

". . . in principle," she continued, her tone suddenly sharp, "but I watched every inch of that station from my side here. There wasn't any sign at all of a name."

Felicity twittered cheerfully and gave a little clap of her hands with excitement. "You see?" she goaded Staymore, "I told you. I told you!"

The Reverend Sullivan Staymore did not speak. He prayed. Jesus, he implored, give me strength to hold back my righteous anger; help me stay my vengeance on these Samaritan swine, for I would smite their heads together till the skulls broke and the brains ran out upon the floor. Then they would not mock your holy minister. Oh no—not him who even You gave the keys to the kingdom of heaven.

"What does it matter what the station was called anyway?" Bill Armstrong said placatingly. "At least it wasn't Faversham!" And he looked pointedly at the sleeping man and then at Ann Cross and tried a grin.

Judas! Staymore thought. Betrayer! This was the unkindest cut of all. For he saw the eyes of the young man move over the legs of the woman and he saw the look that came into them and his sycophantic smile—and he saw that the woman noticed these things also and knew what was in the young man's mind—and scorned him for it. Staymore was hurt and he was sickened. Satan had triumphed before his very eyes. He looked out the window. And then, in his pain, the Law of the Lord gave him comfort. For he remembered that those who coveted and those who seduced and those who lied and mocked the Lord's anointed would all—as sure as that sky out there was overcast and grey —most assuredly rot and writhe in the most terrible torments of hell.

He smiled to himself. And wished them to it.

By his side the scruffy man slept on.

And next to him, in turn, Dr. Robert Latimer's mind was in its limbo place.

But on the opposite seat, Felicity Latimer frothed with excitement. Baiting the priest had been wonderful, his anger thrilling. She sensed she had almost brought him to breaking-point and that he would then have erupted in magnificent, berserk action. Like a mad elephant. He even had the tiny blazing evil eyes of an elephant. She wished, desperately wished, he had run amock. She had a vivid picture of him reaching out to the sleeping man by his side and just tearing the head off his shoulders. Easily. Like a strong man might pluck the head off a chicken. She squirmed a little at the thought of that. Sweet Satan, he was fantastic! Oh yes! She wanted to crawl over him, rub her body along him, sharply drag all the nails of her hands down through his bristly leathered cheeks. She wanted to fill her mouth with the immense sausage fingers of his hands—and gnaw. But the intensity of her feeling robbed her for a time of speech and movement and she sat dumbly, like a paralysed person, staring from under half-lowered eyes at the black-robed figure of the titanic priest—and all her senses throbbed out to him.

And then, like the sound down a long passage of a door closing that is too far away to see, came a memory: the third gate in the trap was down. Behind them. How many more could there be? She looked out to the greying landscape. It was unrolling its sameness faster than ever now. The compartment was swaying and rattling with speed.

Not too many more.

And then?

She looked a bit at the others there. They didn't seem to have any suspicions yet. Her father was in his usual living-dead sort of trance. She wondered why he'd bothered to talk to the woman some while back. And the woman herself—something about her had changed. She was giving off a different sort of aura now. Confused and less sure. Her skirt was showing quite a lot of her legs and she didn't seem to notice. There was a chink in the aura she had out around her and it was opening. Of course it might be just a trap. Like the plants that lure in insects and then close around and dissolve them. She didn't know who the trap might be for, but she did know she wasn't going to go and walk into it herself. She thought it might be for her father. She'd have liked to have seen him caught like a fly in a sticky web and squirming—but she knew he wouldn't be. Though the trap was probably set for her father, the man on her left was far more likely to blunder into it. She'd felt him looking over her head at the woman—sort of unpicking her with his eyes. But Felicity knew he was stupid and the woman could eat him up any time she wanted to. And that also would be good to see. There were so many things happening on this journey, it was fantastic!

At which point, she felt she had to look out of the window.

She wasn't sure what compelled her to. But something did. Forcefully. A feeling. Yes. A feeling very like the one she had once when she had gone with her father to London and, standing outside a big shop in a busy street, had a sudden compulsion to turn—and look. She had. She had looked out into the street. And a young man in a sports car had shot a traffic light and hit a woman fair and square and his car had finally stopped with what was left of her neatly beneath it. It was that feeling Felicity had now as she stared out of the window.

Nothing happened.

She looked and was surprised that it seemed a much gloomier day than before and she was pleased about that—she loved days when it seemed as if the sky was all dribbling away like wax onto a plate—but otherwise there was nothing. Just empty, bleak country with bristly grass that looked sort of spikier than grass usually was. It was slashing and prickling about in the wind like pigmy spear tips. Poisoned spear tips. But that was all. She was disappointed. She'd expected something dramatic. And though the country did have a kind of savage look to it now, it was hardly really dramatic like the woman getting it from the car. That had really been something!

Her instinct had let her down. Felicity felt cheated. And then it started to happen. But for a time she wasn't even aware that it had. And even when she realised this was it, she couldn't say what it was about it that made it matter anyhow.

The land moving by outside was flat. Wide. It stretched away everywhere into distance. Coming from nowhere. Going to nothing. Just land. And it was empty apart from their train and the wind.

And then the dogs.

Across the wide flat void they came running. Just a pack of dogs. From the compartment, it was hard to see what sort of dogs they were. Except that they weren't all the same, were mixed breeds. And they ran bunched close and hard. Bristle-backed. Running as fast as they could. Their tendons strained and jaws were open—but she heard no sound except the train. And whether the dogs fled in fear or in pursuit towards the grey horizon, it was impossible to say.

Though she could not explain it, for the second time since entering the compartment, Felicity Latimer felt the hackles rise along her spine. This time it didn't make her feel good.

Clackety-clack.

Again. Soon. It came so soon she was numb. And then, after a little while, from somewhere she heard her own voice tossing a rhyme up like a coin in her brain:

> "Clackety-clack, clackety-clack
> The wheels are singing with the railroad track
> If you go
> You don't come back."

CHAPTER 11

WELL, well, Bill thought, old tough-nut over there is showing some leg! Not a great deal maybe—but what she's showing is nice. Still, it's probably not deliberate. No? A woman that controlled doesn't do anything without a reason. But what? Maybe she's trying to appeal to someone in the compartment. Hey, yeah! And that couldn't be anyone else but him. An interesting thought! He looked at her again. Of course, she wasn't exactly Miss Universe but on the other hand she wasn't any pig, either. He decided he'd do her a favour.

He smiled at her.

She was facing in his direction and a smile played vaguely about her lips as she looked back at him. Good. He'd chat her up. Then he might buy her a drink in the buffet car—several drinks. And then . . . who knows? Yes, he might do all right

133

there. His only problem would be time. The journey took an hour and twenty minutes to Dover and Bill Armstrong didn't need to look at his watch to know that at least half of that must already be gone. He'd better start with the chat right now. Before she changed her tune and went back to giving him the cold-shoulder she had at the start of the journey.

Bill lifted his jaw a little. Smiled rakishly. Gave a quick deep cough to clear his throat to speak. She looked his way at that. He flicked a curl off his forehead, twitched his lips in a mean sardonic lady-killing kind of way he had—and opened them to speak.

He couldn't think of anything to say.

She looked at him. He stared back at her, mouth open, speech-less. More surprised at himself than anything else. He'd never been at a loss for words before. Now he was like a man who wakes in the morning to blackness, thinks it's still night, turns on the light—and finds he is blind. Bill gaped; struggled to ar-ticulate, to remember what he had been going to say. As if to remind himself he looked at her legs. She followed his gaze. And pulled down her skirt. At that moment he found his voice.

"Uh," he said.

"Yes?"

"Don't have the time, do you?" It was the only thing he could think of.

"I'm afraid my watch has stopped."

"Oh."

"I presume yours has as well?" Dryly she indicated the Omega large on Bill's wrist.

Smoothly Bill turned the dial down into his lap and began to undo the watch strap. "Yes, damn it! They wear these watches to the moon and back without any problems at all—and mine goes and stops on a train!" He knew perfectly well his watch couldn't have stopped, of course, but wasn't going to look at it to find out that. Taking it off his wrist he dropped it quickly in a pocket.

"Can't bear to wear a watch that doesn't go," he said.

"No," Ann Cross said, looking at him wryly.

134

"Normally," he went on, "I could tell the time within a minute or two from the position of the sun . . ." He waited fractionally for her to comment. She didn't, so he continued quickly. "But today—well!" He nodded a head to indicate the sunless day outside.

She looked past him out the window. "It isn't nice, is it?"

"Awful," he agreed.

The little girl by his side, who up to now had been staring into space, now turned her head and looked up at him.

"It must always be like that, here," she said.

Rubbish, Bill thought. The kid's unhinged. He smiled dismissively at her and looked for confirmation of his feeling to the woman. But she didn't seem to have heard and was staring out past him with an absorbed expression. Bill followed her gaze.

Ugh! It was a spooky landscape to see out of the window of a British train, all right. Maybe it was some trick of the light—though, God knows, there wasn't too much of that—but the land now looked so barren, so alien, it could almost have been another world—at the least Death Valley, Bill thought. It was enough to give you the creeps. He looked back into the compartment.

"I expect it'll be a nicer weather where you're going—what?" He smiled at Ann Cross.

For a moment she didn't look at him. The morbid scenery seemed to have a fascination for her. Then slowly she turned her face to him and said coolly: "We might have the window shut, don't you think."

"Sure!"

Bill reached up and shut the partition window. It slid into place with a solid permanent click. He turned to her and smiled reassuringly. "How's that?"

"Thank you."

"As I was saying—I hope it'll be more cheerful where you're off to, eh?"

"I hope so."

By now Bill felt in command of the situation. The woman wasn't exactly making romantic overtures, but at least she was

135

being civil and he was sure that once the old Armstrong chat got under way, everything else would follow in time. Suavely, he went on:

"And where *are* you going . . . Miss Cross?"

He'd expected her to react when he suddenly used her name. He was disappointed. Perhaps her eyes narrowed slightly. But, if so, that was all. When she replied, her manner was as poised as ever.

"Paris. For a while."

That was the point she should have asked him where he was going. But she didn't. Still—he wouldn't be put off by something like that. He had the bit between his teeth now—and anyhow what else was there to do on this lousy train?

"*Paris?* Really! Super city. I've got lots of friends there. I wonder if— Hey, you don't know the Count of Richleau by any chance do you?"

"No."

Bill wasn't surprised at that. He'd just made the man up. It seemed the sort of name the right person to know in Paris should have. He was feeling in good form now, and rather creative. He'd so impress her with his acquaintanceship with the European set that in no time at all she'd be eating out of his hand.

"No?" Bill repeated. "Oh, thought you might. Old Richie's a great friend of mine actually. One of the oldest titles in France, but what an eccentric! Do you know—one year, after dropping a fortune on the turf—he turned over his entire stud farm, one of the finest in all France, entirely to breeding *ostriches!* He actually races 'em, too. When I asked him about it, he just said: 'Bill, lad, racing's strictly for the *birds!*'"

Bill wasn't sure if he hadn't gone a bit far on that one. And it struck him that he hadn't been that funny, either, so her reaction came as quite a surprise. She started to laugh. Heartily. Leaning back in her seat. She's laughing a lot, Bill thought, too much. She isn't far from hysteria. He watched her and began to feel slightly alarmed but then the woman suddenly noticed the doctor opposite and abruptly ceased, and she looked surprised herself that she'd laughed so hard—surprised and worried. "Yes. Well . . ." Bill began again.

"What's an ostrich?"

It was the little girl. Bill glanced down at her annoyed, did not reply, and looked back at Ann. "That was just *one* of Bertie's little foibles," he went on.

"What's an ostrich?" Felicity Latimer repeated.

Bill ignored her determinedly. "You don't by any chance know Guy Montparnasse, do you?" he asked Ann.

"The banker?"

"The polo player."

"What's an ostrich?"

Bill stared down lovelessly at the little girl. Coldly stared into the wide whiteness of her eyes—and suddenly felt a sense of vertigo, like all at once finding himself on a small space wide open with emptiness all around him and a drop with no end below. But he caught on to his anger and that steadied him. He saw that she was looking at him curiously, almost as if she were holding back a smile. Brat, he thought, with those tapeworm lips and weird eyes, she'd do just great in a vampire film.

"Didn't anyone ever tell you?" Bill told her. "You shouldn't interrupt people. It's rude."

"So's talking over people's heads," she countered.

Surprised at first, Bill couldn't help grinning a little at that. He had to hand it to the kid. She was sharp and gutsy. He didn't like her any the more, but he sort of admired her. It was too bad she wasn't eight years older.

"Okay," he shrugged, "the ostrich . . . ?"

"Yes."

"It's a bird. A big bird. It's got gangly legs, a big round body like an egg, and a long neck. It can't fly, but it can run all right. It's very stupid."

"Is that the one that buries its head in the ground and won't look at things when it's scared?"

"Yes!"

"Ostrich!"

She said it loud. She was looking across at the priest and Bill wasn't sure if she was calling him that—or just exclaiming the word. The kid was as weird as they come. But the priest didn't take any notice. Wobbling with the movement of the train, his bristled jowls were fixedly aimed towards the window. They did not turn. After some seconds, the little girl gave a shrug of what seemed disappointment and got up and flounced out into the corridor. Good, Bill thought, now he could get back to the business in hand. And just in time. The woman was about to start on one of her magazines again.

"Wonderful thing a child's curiosity, isn't it?" he said bluffly.

"Is it?"

"Well—I mean—if it weren't for curiosity most of the great inventions would never have happened, would they? We'd probably all still be swinging around from the trees!"

She looked at him flat-faced. "Quite possibly," she said. And began to read.

A litany of oaths went through Bill's mind. Where had he gone wrong? It was all that brat's fault. If she hadn't kept interrupting him, he'd have been well away. Too bad. Now he'd started on this woman, he didn't intend to quit. So he'd lost the first two rounds, so what? There were more to come. And he knew what mattered in this sort of contest was laying your opponent out in the last one!

Bill grinned to himself a little at that. It turned his mind back to Sylvia. For a while he thought about her but it made him feel depressed and restless. What he needed right now was a change.

He got up. For a moment considered leaving his briefcase but decided not to risk it and picked it up from the floor and, holding it tight in his hand, walked past Ann Cross—and out into the corridor. He noticed the woman did not look at him as he went by her. He slid shut the compartment door behind him. Still she did not look up. Ah well . . . it felt good to be stretching his legs again, anyhow. And it was just as well they were fit and his sense of balance good, Bill thought, for the train seemed to be moving like a cavalry charge and lurching round all over the place and a lesser man might have had to hold hard to the rail by the window as he moved up the corridor. As it was, Bill swung easily like a sailor with the swing of the train as he walked up towards the engine, passed two compartments, and came to a toilet. Ah! He opened its door.

And was suddenly seized with uneasiness.

He shut the door behind him; locked it. The uneasiness intensified. There was something wrong. What was worse—he wasn't sure what. And then he suddenly had it. And he gave a sort of laugh of relief and at the same time was aware that he was starting to sweat.

There hadn't been anyone in the compartments.

That wasn't anything to get a man rattled, he reasoned to himself. The rest of the train had been so jam-packed that obviously everyone had got in there. And the next carriage after this was the engine anyhow. Besides, what was so strange about two empty compartments on a train in the first place? Nothing! Lord, human nature was weird to go and get all spooked—a man like himself—over nothing at all like that. It was downright childish. Sure. Bill swung open the toilet door and sauntered out into the corridor. As he pulled the door shut behind him, its handle slipped in his hand.

Bill Armstrong's palm was wet.

He walked back, swaying less easily with the train, but feeling better as he got to his compartment. Outside its sliding door, he paused. He didn't feel like going in and sitting down just yet. He turned, and, leaning on the handrail of the corridor window, looked out.

It was an awful view.

Chiefly because there was nothing to see—except grey. Ugly land and sky and everything in between were grey. Just that. A surrealist painting of merging grey shapes—that represented nothing. Bill rubbed a hand across the window-pane. Near the bottom, it seemed to have condensation and he tried to clear it. But it wasn't on the glass. It was outside—a mist rising from barren earth, a swirling ground mist. To a wild imagination it was not unlike volcanic smoke. But Bill didn't have a wild imagination and all he saw was steaming cold mist rising and coalescing into fog that gradually thickened and blotted out the dreary landscape and climbed up towards the sky.

The sky itself was about as cheerful as leprosy. Scabby and suppurating. That sky was not something Bill delighted to watch —for, momentarily as he did so, he felt himself drawn up into its swirling dark reaches and he was the size of a pin up there and on every side of him rolled nothingness. Eternal. And afraid.

Bill turned away from the window and went back to his compartment.

The woman was reading and took no notice of him. The priest looked fixedly out of the window. The scruffy man slept. The doctor's eyes were closed. The little girl was still gone. The scene was just as he had left it. Nothing had altered. And that struck Bill as strange. For in his own world in the last few minutes so much time had gone by.

He sat, his briefcase on his lap, and looked at the woman. She was reading composedly, skirt demurely below her knee and Bill sensed that for the rest of the journey that was where it would stay; that whether her little exhibition had been deliberate or not, it wouldn't be repeated. For some reason this filled him with a sense of slight desperation and an urgency and determination to win over this woman that was out of all proportion to her attraction. Almost as if something in his subconscious was telling him that there wasn't much time. And he must fill it to the best of his capacity.

"I say!" Bill said.

No one took any notice of him.

"Miss Cross?" he directed himself to Ann.

She didn't move her eyes from her magazine. "Yes?"

"You were telling me about your trip to Paris. Where were we?"

"Nowhere."

"Hah! I tell you one place we're certainly not—and that's the tropics, eh?" Bill nodded towards the window.

Ann Cross glanced up at him fleetingly, her expression distaste. "Quite," she said.

140

"You know," Bill chuckled, "I'd say the driver's lost his way —and's taking us to Antarctica!" He laughed at his joke.

Ann Cross went back to reading her magazine.

"Miss Cross?"

"What is it?" she questioned wearily without looking up.

"You're a bitch, Miss Cross."

She looked up at that. But not at Bill. She looked to the men on the opposite seat. It was only when she saw that the priest ignored her, the man beside him slept, and beside him in turn, the doctor had his eyes closed, that she faced Bill Armstrong.

"What did you say?" she asked him.

Bill smiled at her, spoke slowly, pronouncing each word with care. "I said you are a bitch. A rude little bitch."

Ann Cross stared in silence into Bill's eyes. He was glad he'd said that but his pleasure was marred as, to his surprise, he found he was unable to tell whether she wanted to scratch his eyes out, or whether his words had left her unmoved. After some seconds, she swung her face towards the man opposite her.

"Doctor!" she said sharply.

Dr. Robert Latimer opened his eyes. There was no sign of sleep in them. He stared at the woman. He opened his mouth. It stayed open some time before he finally spoke.

"Yes?"

Ann Cross looked him over appraisingly. Bill sensed more than saw a hidden sneer behind her scrutiny. She made a gesture towards Bill. "This man's being intolerable," she complained.

"Really? How?"

"Abusive. For no reason at all, he—he called me a *bitch!*"

"*Did* he?"

"Yes!"

"Well now—I'm not qualified to express an opinion on the subject, but—he may perfectly well be right."

Bill could hardly believe the doctor's reply. But the woman's reaction to it was even more surprising. She sneered openly, nodded to herself as if she'd been expecting that precise remark.

"You punk," she told the doctor urbanely.

Dr. Robert Latimer nodded at her slightly, gave a half smile, and closed his eyes. She went on staring at him for some moments. Then she turned towards Bill.

"As for you . . ." she said.

And that was as far as she got. For her look moved from Bill to the window and her voice trailed away. Hah! he thought, she hasn't looked out for some time—and doesn't like what there now is to see. Good. He hoped the view depressed her.

"Why is it like that?" Ann Cross's voice cut into his thoughts. It was strangely bleak, her voice now, he noticed. And it had an edge to it. For a moment he couldn't make out what. Then he realised what that edge was. It was fear. That pleased Bill, gave him a feeling of strength. He turned towards her, spoke confidently, not really thinking about her question or answer.

"It's gravel pits, that sort of thing, you know," he replied—all confident male.

"But it's all the same for so long!" She looked at him now.

Bill couldn't really answer that. "Slag heaps, disused quarries . . ." he began—and then he was saved from having to continue. The priest turned from his vigil at the window.

"This is the sort of light that precedes a total eclipse of the sun," Staymore stated, and turned back to the window.

"Of course, the light creates the effect and has a lot to do with it," Bill went on.

Clackety-clack.

The train lurched violently. So violently, it was amazing they were not derailed. It was if they had jumped a missing section of track. Their compartment tilted sharply to the left. Latimer was thrown against the scruffy man who in turn cannoned into Staymore. Staymore's head hit the thick glass of the window hard. On the facing seat, Bill had his back to the window and Ann Cross was hurled right across the compartment into his arms.

"Ow!"

The exclamation burst from him. And then the train was moving as before and Ann Cross was moving away. Admittedly she had only been there a split second and he hadn't been pre-

142

pared for it—yet there had been nothing nice about her nearness. Strangely, her so soft-seeming body had felt like metal against him. Like the automatons of fiction. Whose impeccable skin is plastic, cool and thin, above steel.

On the opposite seat the tangle of bodies was sorting out. Latimer came off the scruffy man, went back to his place. The scruffy man had woken. Half. "Whuh?" he mumbled, recovering his position. He looked round him blankly, then, squirming his back into his seat, went to sleep once more.

Staymore alone did not move.

His huge frame was slumped. His head still lolled against the window. It juddered against the window with the movement of the train. And blood was on the glass.

Hands fluttering over hair and clothing in instinctive feminine movement, Ann Cross saw Staymore. She caught her breath. For an instant was quite still. Then she turned to Dr. Latimer.

"Help him, you fool—he's bleeding!" she shouted. And Bill, who by now had recovered some of his own composure, was aware of the hysteria in her voice.

Latimer faced her down. Then, slowly, taking his time, he looked across at the priest. At that moment, Staymore's body straightened and his head came away from the window. Amazingly, his glasses were not broken. He turned his face in on the compartment. He was cut around the temple. It was hard to see quite where because there was blood. It welled from the side of his head, like a furry caterpillar, undulated slowly over his bristled cheeks, down over his chins to his sweat-soaked ecclesiastical collar. His blood was thick and dark.

He smiled through it at the compartment.

His smile was loose. The woman sucked in her breath when she saw it and turned away. Bill noticed that she had the little finger of her left hand in her mouth and was biting the nail.

"You all right?" Latimer asked the priest disinterestedly.

"Fine, my dear, fine." Staymore beamed.

"You don't want me to look at your head?"

"My head?"

"It's cut."

143

Staymore put a hand to his skull, felt the blood there, drew away his fingers and looked at the blood on them. He peered at the doctor cunningly: "Just a scratch as they say, eh?"

"As you say."

"Ah!"

Staymore took a handkerchief from his robes then and mopped at his head. Already it was bleeding less. "I think a little cold water," he announced. He rose. "Excuse me," he said to the scruffy man—now once more fast asleep—and left the compartment.

Bill turned his attention back to Ann Cross. She looked vacant and a little shocked. Right—this was the moment to get the ball rolling again.

"Good old British Rail!" He was surprised his voice had a slight tremble. He corrected it. "You can always rely on 'em to turn a journey to the coast into a battlefield!"

"What happened?"

"We probably ran over a cow or something."

"Oh."

"You know, I'd say all this excitement calls for a drink. Can I offer you one?"

"You won't get a drink on this train!"

It was Felicity Latimer. She stood swaying in the doorway left open by the priest's departure. She was smiling. Quietly. To herself. A smile of knowledge that she alone had—and would not share. Bill looked up at her angrily.

"Belt up!" he said to her curtly, then to Ann, "Well?"

Ann looked at him, looked at the black-haired little girl still smiling in the compartment doorway.

"No."

She turned her face once more to her magazine. Felicity flounced into the compartment and sat down. Bill looked away from her angrily out the window.

Three strange people—so much so they were almost interesting, thought Dr. Latimer. None more than his daughter. She was up to something now that was sordid or criminal. Possibly both. He could tell from the air of suppressed excitement about

144

her. He hoped that, whatever it was, it would not be messy. Life bored him but he liked it to be neat. This journey now wasn't neat. But it had the advantage of being bizarre. The people, normal-looking enough, were not behaving normally. And the view from the window now was rather what he imagined a cancerous lung must look like. From the inside. Flaky, sheeny mist was everywhere. Tangible, palpable, it coiled and coalesced into thick substantial fog. There was little indication of what sort of landscape it shrouded. Spongy greyness was all. It even penetrated inside the compartment, Dr. Latimer noticed, casting a speckly leprous grey on the flesh and features of the people there, giving their skin the colour and texture of people in a hot country some days dead.

He reached up and turned on the light.

As he did so, he saw his daughter's self-satisfaction vanish. She had noticed the priest was no longer in his place. It clearly upset her. Why this preoccupation with the "Holy Man"? Latimer wondered vaguely. The attraction of opposites—or like to like? Either way it didn't matter. About this, or anything else, he couldn't really care less.

"Where's he gone?" Felicity demanded of Bill.

Bill turned his head more firmly to the window.

"Where is he?"

Bill spun round at Latimer. The doctor noticed his fists were clenched. "Look you—Doctor whatever you're called," Bill almost shouted, "why don't you keep this kid of yours under some sort of control, huh?"

This man is angry, Latimer thought, and possibly violent. He is clearly strong. Latimer did not like pain. That is, were he experiencing it himself. He looked half-apologetically at Bill and shrugged.

"By all means feel free yourself to try," he said politely. And he closed his eyes.

Punk twerp! Bill fumed. It was clear what this kid needed— a damn good spanking. He wished he had it in him to give it to her. But he knew he could never hit a woman or a child.

"Well?" Felicity asked—looking amused that there had been a fuss about her.

"Well what?" Bill scowled.

"Where is he?"

"I'm going to tell you this once, love, and I'm not going to repeat myself. *Shut up.* You pester me any more and I warn you, I'll put you over my knee and give you a hiding."

"Splendid!" said the Reverend Sullivan Staymore.

He was standing huge in the doorway. The blood was gone from his temple, which showed a livid weal. He beamed at Bill—who did not smile back at him. Felicity herself had been poised to answer Bill. Instead she turned towards the doorway and said in scolding tone:

"I thought you'd gone."

"Gone? Gone where?" Staymore queried, moving in and sitting.

At which Felicity just smiled—smiled a secret smile to herself—and did not reply.

Bloody weirdos, Bill thought. The whole morbid mob of 'em have flipped. Someone ought to come along and scoop up the lot of them and put them in a home. The taste of them and the fog outside was tacky in his mouth. He needed a strong double gin to wash it out. Yeah—and if that frosty red-headed effort wouldn't drink with him, he'd damn well drink alone. He'd been wise, too, he reflected, not to have left his briefcase with all the money in it on the seat when he'd gone out before. This lot was so freaky that for all he knew they might have opened it up and eaten it.

Bill held his briefcase tight in his hand and stood. He walked to the door. Two paces from it, he saw the woman's feet and had a sudden inspiration to step on her toes—as if by accident. But she must have been watching from under her down-turned eyes, for as his foot descended towards one of hers she moved her legs. Bill stepped on only floor, and his impetus carried him on out of the compartment.

His failure to achieve his inspiration of stubbing her toes didn't leave him in a very sweet temper and he slammed shut the compartment door behind him. For a tiny fraction of time —about as long as it took for his hand to leave the door and his body to turn and face down the corridor—Bill felt simply angry. But even as he took his first steps away from the compartment, his anger died; he was walking the opposite way to his last excursion but once again had that same feeling of unidentifiable unease. Two steps. He was aware that, though the train moved, if anything, faster than ever as it hurtled through the fog-obscured countryside, the air along the corridor seemed motionless. Was close and thick. And still.

Three steps.

He was moving by the neighbouring compartment. He passed it. As he did so, he turned his head. Looked in.

At no one.

The impact of it hit him before he reached the second compartment. Not fully. But enough to slow his feet so that he came upon that compartment at a leisurely pace—and had plenty of time to see that it too was empty.

Just past the second compartment, Bill stopped, remembered. Both these had been crammed when he got on the train. Now they looked as dustily unused as if they'd never held anyone at all. There were no signs of habitation: no baggage, overcoats, newspapers. Most important—no people. He tried to reason it out. It was possible some could have gone to the toilet and others to have a drink or look at the view. It was possible. Not much more. There wasn't any view now, apart from thick oppressive fog. It was unlikely that the entire compartment would want to go to the john simultaneously. And even if some were there and others at the bar, or all of them at the bar, people didn't usually take all their belongings with them when they went for a gin and tonic. Of course, if the train had stopped, there wouldn't be anything strange in the situation. Only it hadn't. Where had they gone? Bill wondered desperately. And then he had it— the only possible answer—to another compartment! He realised he should feel relieved. He wasn't. He didn't see why the people should want to move. It was unpleasantly like rats and a sinking ship.

Bill didn't want to be the rat that got left behind.

Not reassured, he started to walk again. He didn't want to. He was afraid of what he would see. He saw it. The third compartment also was empty.

This is silly, Bill thought with the anger of deepening fear. He walked faster. Faster, as he passed yet another compartment. Another. He was almost running when he got to the end of the carriage. He stopped abruptly. Breathing fast. The communicating door that separates railway coaches was closed. He put out a hand to sweep it open, but his sweating palm froze on the chill metal. He could not make himself open the door. Behind him the entire carriage, all its eight compartments, had been empty, the people he'd previously seen there as if they had never been. That was behind him. He did not want to see what was in front. He no longer wanted a drink. He stood for a time with his hand on the handle. Then he took it away. He stood there. He did not think much. He did not do anything. He stood there.

He did not know why, did not care why—he was sweating, stupid, with fear.

Propelled by a homing instinct more than anything else, he turned and took two slow steps back towards his compartment. At which point, there was a snap of metal, a dry wind on his back. The communicating door slammed open behind him.

Bill Armstrong jumped with shock. He darted three fast steps—when the train lurched. He stumbled and fell. He fell on his face. He scrambled to get to his feet. The train lurched again and threw him sideways and he fell onto the floor on his back —facing the way he had come.

There was nothing and no one there.

Bill sat on the railway corridor floor and realised that and felt weak with relief. He saw he still clutched his briefcase in his left hand. He patted it and laughed a little with quiet, rather uneven laughter. Then he became aware of where he was and got carefully to his feet and leaned against a corridor window and dusted himself off as best he could. He began to feel a fool. What on earth had made him so jumpy? He looked at the communicating door. It was sliding forwards and back on its rail with the

148

movement of the train. Through it, round a slight corner—and he would see a long and empty carriage. Blandly identical, he knew, to the one he was in. He turned away. He didn't want to see that carriage. His relief had gone. He found he wanted to sprint down the passage. It was hard not to—but he made himself walk slowly, deliberately slowly, back to his compartment. It was insane, he knew, but he was frightened that somehow it might not be there.

But, of course, it was.

Bill opened its door like a man who wakes to a sunny morning after a nightmare. He had an urge to grin at everyone there and declare cheerfully: "Well, here I am! Back from the wars all safe and sound!" It was only when he'd closed the door and was moving to his seat that he realised the bad dream was not over, that it had only begun. For, with the exception of the scruffy man who still slept, every face in that tiny rattling room was turned towards the window. And their petrified stillness was that of people turned to salt.

Outside their window, just above the fog, swung a corpse on a gibbet.

CHAPTER 12

IT wasn't possible.

That was Bill Armstrong's first thought after his mind unfroze from shock and the skin ceased prickling cold down his spine. It wasn't possible. And yet—it was. It was there. It was hard to say how far away. It was the only distinguishable shape in a sea of grey that rolled with the unending denseness of a cloud plateau seen from a plane above. But there wasn't any doubt it was there. Jutting up through the fog like the top-mast of an ancient schooner. Perhaps it was only a tree or a telegraph pole. But then, what was the object that dangled from it? Though the fog writhed around it and the light was dim, and though the train was moving fast away, Bill Armstrong wasn't in any doubt what that object was. It was a corpse. Hanging by its stretched-out neck. Limp and dead. And dripping into the fog.

Bill stumbled to his seat, dropped his case on the floor, sat down, pressed his face to the window. As he did so, the fog wrapped around the object. And it soon became apparent that he would not see it again.

"What on earth was that?" he said, turning from the glass with an attempt at cheerfulness.

Staymore looked at Bill. His blubbery face was grim. For an instant his huge arms juddered in his lap, with reflex twitches like a rabbit that kicks in spasms after death. Then they were still and he leaned forward confidentially. He smiled a smile that did not part his lips.

"Don't worry, my dear," he said, reaching across and placing a huge hand on Bill's knee and squeezing it.

"But he should!" Felicity twittered.

"I'm not worrying," Bill snapped, pushing Staymore's hand from his leg, "I just want to know what that—that—thing was."

"It was a corpse," Dr. Latimer said.

For a moment, the flatness, the certainty of his tone silenced them all. They looked at the doctor's impassive, unexpressive face.

"Don't be so stupid," Bill suddenly snapped.

"I'm not."

"Oh? What makes *you* so sure?" Ann Cross asked contemptuously.

"I'm a doctor. I have seen the dead before."

"Oh?"

"I expect that's how most of your patients end up."

"You're very abusive."

"And you're a fool."

"You honestly think you see corpses just hanging round the British countryside, do you?" Bill mocked.

"Huh!" Ann Cross sneered.

"Huh!" Bill repeated.

"Do you think this looks like the British countryside?" Latimer asked Bill calmly.

Bill glanced briefly at the window, looked quickly away. The doctor was right—damn him!

"Man's nuts," Bill turned and said to Ann.

"I couldn't agree with you more!" she replied.

"You should take care, young man."

"Oh yeah? Who of—you?"

"That's a joke!" Ann sneered.

"And how!" Bill said.

"Not him. Of where we're *going!*" Felicity trilled.

"I warned you—" Bill began, but Staymore interrupted him.

"You're upset, my dear," the priest said sympathetically.

"Upset?" Bill repeated, "Jesus! What would you be after gaping at—at—that?"

"An optical illusion," Staymore pronounced disapprovingly.

"Oh sure. And I had another one out in the corridor also, I suppose. Well, you may all be mad, but I'm *not*. And maybe it might just interest you to know that all the people in that whole lousy carriage out there have just got spirited away. Perhaps you'd care to explain *that!*"

Clackety-clack.

The compartment shook hard once again. Felicity gave a little gasp of delight. "We're in it now!" she exclaimed. But no one took any notice of her. They were staring at Bill.

"That's right," he went on savagely. "There's no one in this entire carriage but us. Not a single damned soul!"

"No one else in the carriage, eh?" Staymore was thoughtful.

"That's right!"

"And what, my dear, is so upsetting about that?"

"Didn't you see it when you got on? It was bloody packed out!"

"Stop swearing!"

"There wasn't a free seat anywhere!"

"I think you'll find there's a perfectly ordinary explanation."

"No, there isn't." Felicity giggled. "Not ordinary!"

"Why must you always interrupt, child!" Staymore grunted angrily.

"Because I *know*—that's why!" she preened. "I know . . ."

"Shut up—blast you!" Bill breathed through clenched teeth.

"My son!" Staymore exclaimed.

"No," Felicity replied. "I shan't."

"I'm warning you . . ."

"You can't make me, either!"

Bill must have been much more worked up than he knew, for the next moment he was on his feet high above the child and his fist was drawn back and clenched tight before her face.

"Go on—hit me! I dare you! I dare you!"

But Bill didn't hit her, for a huge hand came up behind him and caught his wrist. "Calm yourself," the voice of the Reverend Staymore spoke in his ear—and then the tension went out of him. As he felt it slumping out of him, he thought: maybe I really wasn't going to hit her anyway.

"Spoil-sport!" Felicity pouted at Staymore.

He ignored her. Holding Bill by the elbow, he urged him gently towards the door. "Let's go and look into this thing together, shall we, my dear?" he murmured into Bill's ear.

Bill nodded. He preceded Staymore to the compartment door. Reaching it, in an automatic moment of manners, he tried to stand aside for the priest. But Staymore impatiently waved a hand for him to go first—and he did.

Outside in the corridor, all numbness left Bill's mind and he was afraid once more. It was darker there and as he looked through the corridor window, fog was all he could see. He was aware of the priest standing close by him, looking at it also. He heard him give an involuntary snort of disgust—and then he suddenly smelt the overpowering sweet body smell of the man's sweating flesh and it made his gorge rise and he moved away. As he did so, he glanced into the compartment he had just left. It seemed a bright cocoon of warmth and light. He wanted to be back in it. But the priest was following him now, his huge body filling the passage behind him, and more to avoid the man than anything else, Bill moved away up the corridor.

In the speckled grey light from the fog they moved up the rattling corridor of the speeding train: Bill Armstrong with the priest close behind him, too close for Bill's peace of mind. And as Bill had done alone, they passed compartment after compartment and all were empty of people or anything that belonged to them.

Bill stopped at the end of the carriage and looked round at Staymore. The massive priest blocked the passageway. His eyes, behind his thick-lensed glasses, looked like pellets of mud. His jowls were quivering. His face so gleamed with sweat that it resembled a lump of heavily salted grey meat, sparkling as it decomposed in the sun. It was impossible to know what the brain behind that face was thinking.

Bill stared at him with open disgust. "Satisfied?" he sneered.

"Strange," Staymore murmured thoughtfully.

"You're telling me it's strange!"

"No doubt they have transferred carriages."

"No doubt."

"Let's go and see, shall we?"

Bill didn't want to go on. He wanted to be clear of the stink of the huge man towering over him. He wanted to be back in the compartment. He wanted a drink. Most of all, he suddenly realised, he violently wanted to be somewhere else. Anywhere —as long as it wasn't here. God, did he! But the priest was suddenly moving towards him with the relentlessness of a boulder starting down a slope and, unless he wanted to get flattened against the communicating door, Bill saw he didn't have any option but to go on.

He did.

With Staymore lowering close to him, he slid back the door. It was stiff and required almost all his strength to move. He couldn't understand how it had managed to slide itself open when he had stood there before. But he didn't have much time to wonder about that. Staymore was crowding after him and he passed through into the next carriage. Crossing the articulated link section between carriages, he looked down at the steel floor slats. He saw through them a little, saw only darkness hurtling by beneath the train.

Bill strode quickly on. He passed a toilet. It was vacant. He

154

passed the first compartment. It was empty. He stopped then and turned to face Staymore. The priest was close behind him.

"There isn't going to be anyone in this one either," Bill said.

"Don't be silly!" Staymore came up to him. "Go on." He pushed Bill on the shoulder.

"Lay off!" Bill glared at the huge man. "Keep your hands to yourself—see?"

Staymore's glasses sparkled across at Bill and he smiled his sticky-lipped smile. And Bill was suddenly scared. The fat freak gave him the creeps. He wasn't sure which he feared most —the priest, or what he was going to find on this life-forsaken coffin of a train.

He walked on. Fast. What he was looking for didn't take time to see. He saw it in every compartment he went by. Nothing. The compartments were each identical, like animated rattling exhibits in some future museum—"railway compartments circa 1970." Only the museum caretaker should have gotten fired, for they looked too dusty and unused ever to have been real. And their present and total emptiness seemed more their natural state than any absurd notion that they had, or ever could have, held people.

Bill was almost at a run by the time he got to the end of the corridor. It gave him a shock to see, as he spun round, that Staymore was right behind him.

"So I was silly, was I?" Bill snarled.

"My dear, your attitude is." Staymore was panting slightly. "If everyone who walked through an empty coach reacted as you do, British Rail would be responsible for a considerable number of nervous breakdowns!" He smirked.

Bill couldn't help himself snapping back. "You smug simpering fool!" he spat. "You don't understand, do you? Well, you'll see soon enough!"

Without waiting for the priest's reaction, Bill spun round and went on into the next carriage down the train. He was very angry. Very scared. Jangled nerves, half memories, intuitions, dreams, threshed under his skin and told him . . . horror. Just that. He plunged on. Passed empty compartments one after the other. He came to the end of the coach. Into another. This was open-plan. The corridor ran through its centre, stretching tight down it, with seats on either side. It was possible to see at a glance that the entire carriage was empty.

The train was racketing from side to side, making a feverish pace, but as best he could Bill hurried along the swaying gangway; and then, three-quarters way down the aisle between the seats, he suddenly felt alone. There was no sound, no sense of presence behind him, nothing but the clatter of the infernal train. God, where was the priest? Bill stopped and whirled round. The answer almost hit him in the face. Staymore was waddling hugely long-strided, close behind him, and, having got his bulk to speed, did not stop easily.

Bill grunted mixed-feelingly: relieved not to be alone, abhorring the company he had. He went quickly on—and now, knowing that the man was there, he fancied he could feel him breathing all down the back of him and the priest's breath seemed hot and sticky and enveloping, like the tongue of a massive beast sliming on his neck.

Through towards another compartment.

A Pullman car. Here, if anywhere, they would be—all the people somehow gone from their seats. Hope dies hard. As he reached out to slide back the door, Bill imagined he could hear voices from the other side of it and in his mind with sudden relief he pictured a coach surgingly full of people taking morning coffee and ignoring each other and reading newspapers and doing everything that people normally did in a nice normal train.

Bill slid back the door. He was right about the places set for morning coffee. White table-clothed, white-lamped, they had all the antiseptic unappetisingness of British Rail eating cars. Only maybe they looked more unappetising—simply because there wasn't anyone sitting at them.

Bill stopped in the doorway, gagged there. Staymore came up behind him and pushed him into the Pullman and followed him through—and then he also stopped and looked and took in the fact that it was empty.

"Interesting," he said.

Sure, Bill thought, about as interesting as having one's head cut off.

He suddenly shuddered. "It's the *Marie Celeste* again!"

"Rubbish."

"Yes. It's just like it—the ship they found with everything happening on it, kettles even boiling on the stove, but no one there."

"The *Marie Celeste* was a hoax."

"Hah! And what's this? I suppose the people are all really all around us—but we just can't see them. *Very* likely!"

Staymore smiled at Bill benignly. "You're not being very rational, my dear," he said.

"Screw rational. This is a ghost train, I tell you!"

"Really?" Staymore was supercilious.

"A train of the dead," Bill continued with a shudder.

"Ah! Then what are *we?*" He reached out a blubbery hand and, without warning, squeezed Bill's cheek. "Presumably you feel that, do you?" He smiled as Bill jerked from his hand. "Ah—you do! That could be because you're alive. I suggest, therefore, that you reserve your judgement, such as it is, until we have inspected the rest of the train. You see, perhaps I shouldn't say this, but the age of miracles is past. For everything in this world there is a perfectly rational explanation."

Bill glowered at him.

"Perhaps you'd care to lead on?" Staymore gestured.

Bill didn't much care if he did or he didn't. Dazed and heavy with foreboding, he turned—and obeyed.

They were efficient as they searched the rest of the train. But instinctively Bill knew they didn't have to be—that there wasn't anything to find. Nonetheless, they looked into every compartment, every toilet, buffet car, luggage van, cupboard, cubby-hole, socket—aperture small enough to hold no more than a rat.

But they didn't find a rat. They found nothing. Not a steward. Not a guard. Not a passenger. Not a ticket collector. It seemed that Bill Armstrong was right: they were the only life on the train.

In the final empty carriage, Bill turned and confronted Staymore. He felt sick. "So there's a simple explanation is there?" he sneered at the huge man.

Staymore had a smile on his sweating face. He nodded slowly. With complacency he said: "Of course."

"Oh, yeah?"

"There was never anyone here in the first place."

"Jesus Christ, man!"

"*Stop* that!"

"Are you blind? You think this train was empty when we all got on it?"

"It must have been," Staymore said dismissively and turned and began to walk back.

At that moment, Bill Armstrong realised he had left his briefcase behind—the briefcase containing over two thousand pounds. Strangely, though, he already felt so sick it didn't seem to matter much and he followed the black bulk of the priest out of the compartment. They walked on. More slowly than they had come. They were about half-way down the corridor of the penultimate coach.

The sliding door smashed shut behind them.

Both men jumped round. Both faces were white. But as they looked back there was only the closed door to see. Bill found he was shaking a little. Perhaps it was cold. Dead cold. He looked out a window. The fog was making shapes. Staymore walked on. Bill looked away from the window and hurried to catch him. He passed through into the third carriage just behind the priest, was only just through the door, when it, too, snapped shut behind him.

Bill faced round, clench-fisted, at the closed door. For a second he stared, paralysed, at its blankness. Then he reached out to its handle to wrench it open. He heaved. It was stuck. He exerted all his strength. The door would not open.

"Hey!" Bill yelled at Staymore over his shoulder.

The priest was half-way down the corridor. He stopped and turned back to face Bill.

"It's locked," Bill said frantically.

Staymore did not reply, but he came up to Bill with a tolerant smile that quite clearly said, "You're talking nonsense." He brushed Bill out of his way and applied his hand to the door. It did not move. He put his weight behind his arm and pulled. Watching him, Bill thought the man had the strength to tear down a tree.

But he couldn't open the door they had just walked through.

Finally, he realised it and gave up. He looked puzzled. Then he turned from the door and walked away. Bill stared after him, stared at the immovable door.

"You see?" he screamed.

But Staymore did not turn and just went walking on.

Staring down the corridor after him, at that moment, Bill saw salvation. The metal communication cord—that would stop the train. It was above a window near the carriage ceiling. He saw it like a man in quicksand sees a lifeline.

"I've had enough of this," he said aloud, trying to think more casually than he felt. He strode to the chain and reached out and yanked it down—so hard he nearly tore it from its metal fastening. He waited then. Wiped some sweat from his forehead. He felt better. Penalty for "improper use," he read above the dangling chain. Hah! No use could be more proper than this.

And then his relief began to fade.

There came no squeal of brakes, no violent slowing, no sense of deceleration at all. If anything, the train rumbled and rattled and clattered still faster. After about a minute, it became clear to Bill that it wasn't going to stop.

He ran.

He came out of a carriage. He saw the priest's back going into the next one. He heard the door behind him snap shut. He ran. Through this carriage. Into the next. Once again, with the door slamming to just after he passed it. Staymore was half-way down this corridor. Bill ran to him. The man was standing looking out of the window into the inpenetrable fog. Bill fumbled to a halt beside him.

"I pulled the stop chain," he gasped. "Nothing happened!"

But Staymore didn't seem to notice that Bill had spoken. He went on looking out and did not turn his head. Bill stared at the man's grey sweating face with hatred—and then he saw the communication cord dangling above it. Used and useless. In his life he had seen no thing so obscene.

Bill backed off a pace. Staymore blocked the corridor. Behind him the door was closed. Unopenable. He was trapped, caged. The sense of claustrophobia was so heavy on him that he felt it crushing down on his shoulders like a falling mine, smothering in on his throat with unbreathable dust. He cast his head around, looked frantically about him, noticed there was an exit door in the corridor. He lurched to it. It was only a yard away. But it had no handle inside the train. It had a pull-down window, though, and if he could open it, he could get at the handle outside the door. He pulled down on the window, tugged at it savagely, hung all his weight on it till he was suspended from the ground by it alone. But it would not come. Bill backed off from it. He felt his chest heaving. He found it hard to keep the door in his line of sight. His eyes kept flicking from left to right, darting up, down, the corridor. He saw but did not see that Staymore was gone. He backed up till his back was pressed against the cold glass of a compartment behind him. He leaned right against that. Then he raised his leg and lashed out with all the strength in it at the window.

It didn't even crack.

But it came away in one entire, unbroken piece, frame and all. And, incredibly, it seemed to hang for a second suspended. Then like a feather, it swirled lightly away and was gone into the fog.

Bill stood, back to the compartment, and looked at the void his foot had made. There was nothing to see in it but greyness; then through it came a rush of cold and rancid air and, even as he watched, tentacles of mist that writhed around the window edges and seemed to be reaching out across the corridor towards him.

Bill knew that he could never put his hand into that moving grey, let alone jump out to its blindness from the speeding train. Back to the opposite side of the corridor, he began to edge away from the window. He went the length of the carriage like this,

160

watching the fog seep in, and only when he was almost at the communicating door did he feel sufficiently far away to turn his back to it.

He darted through the door, shut it quickly behind him, leaned heavily on it—feeling, as much as someone who was still so frightened could, relief.

Then Bill noticed that Staymore had stopped in this carriage also. He was standing half-way along it, looking so much as he had in the previous carriage that for a moment Bill felt he had gone back in time. For, as before, the priest stared vacantly out into blankness. As before, the communication cord dangled impotently above him.

Bill froze where he stood and examined the priest and his every sense told him there was something about the man which yelled danger. Immediate and real and threatening his life. Suddenly he saw what it was. The man's flipped, he thought. Insane. He's smiling out the window like a child at a puppet show. Only there isn't anything there to see.

Bill came up beside him quietly. Staymore's intentness was complete. Bill couldn't help looking out also. There wasn't anything to look at—just featureless fog blanketing around them. That was all. Or was it? Peering harder, now, Bill noticed that the fog appeared in places to be acquiring more substance, its fluidity hardening. Intestines of mist appeared, rolled revoltingly by. And then it seemed to Bill that he saw the shapes of faces— skeletal, leprous white clown faces with gaping whirlpool mouths. And there were swimming things there, too. Slimy and huge. White sharks with eyes of oil pacing the train, threshing just outside the window. In wait.

Bill made himself turn away. Staymore was looking at him. He looked at the priest.

"My dear," Staymore said softly, and then, after a pause, "it seems we are alone on the train!"

He turned face-on to Bill and he spread out his arms. He spanned the corridor. He smiled.

The instinct for self-preservation is a mighty thing. But it is not always well informed. And as easily as it can save a man's life, it can stampede him to suicide. Bill Armstrong hit the Reverend Sullivan Staymore with the hardest right he had ever thrown in his life.

He hit him with science and strength. He hit him with all the training of his days in the ring, all the force of his body and weight. He uppercut him just beneath the heart. It was a punch that could easily have killed a man and the Reverend Sullivan Staymore wasn't ready for it at all.

He went down like a lumberjacked tree.

He jerked up, swayed back onto his heels, toppled straight over backwards. He hit the floor with an impact that shook the corridor. When someone got slammed like that, they didn't hurry any to get up, Bill thought, staring down at the priest with grim satisfaction. But his satisfaction didn't last. For Staymore had hardly been on the floor a second before he started to rise. In a hurry. And, seeing that, Bill Armstrong was an even more frightened man than he had been before. As the priest came up, Bill kicked out as hard as he could at his face. The blow was aimed at the jaw and it carried enough weight and speed behind it to have torn the man's head from his shoulders. Only it didn't hit target. Instead of the jaw, Bill's foot smashed into Staymore's chest just below the collar bone. The priest grunted with pain, was lashed back. He came up again. Bill kicked out again. At his crotch. His foot sank into flesh. The priest gave a bellowing groan and convulsed forward, half-sitting, onto his face. Bill raised his fist and clubbed it down on the back of Staymore's bull-thick neck. The priest desisted from any further efforts to rise then and slumped sideways, face-down, across the passage. Bill stood, panting, and looked down at him. The whole fight could not have lasted a minute. It seemed a lot longer. He'd had the advantage of surprise and attack and unremitting aggression—and he felt very good to have won. There was a time when he thought the priest could not be stopped.

Bill stepped over Staymore's crumpled form, took one further step down the corridor. That was all he took.

A hand was around his ankle.

Bill stood quite still. In the grip of that hand—and of shock.

162

And then, with a heart that was like a tiny trapped animal smashing against the cage of his ribs to get free, he tried to lunge forward to wrench his foot from the restraining hand. But that hand could have been a bear-trap of steel for, though it moved forward some inches with Bill's pull, it didn't loosen its grip at all.

Bill turned and stared in terror over his shoulder. Then he leant all his weight forward and tried to tear loose. He couldn't. He looked back at the priest. He was half-lying, half-sitting, along the floor facing him and holding him with only one hand— the other dangling awkwardly from what Bill desperately hoped was a dislocated shoulder. But his hope was submerged by fear. For Staymore was mad. Through the dust and sweat and the pain on his face, as he looked at Bill, he was smiling.

"That wasn't very friendly," he purred.

Bill turned his back on the priest; to keep his balance, grabbed the handrail; tugged desperately. He managed to move a pace or two down the passage, but he was dragging the priest behind him and he didn't have the strength to tear loose and it seemed like his leg was about to be wrenched apart from his body.

"You mustn't try to go away," Staymore said reproachfully.

Bill looked round at the madman and pleaded. "Oh God— please—look—I didn't mean to—I'm sorry . . ."

Staymore giggled. The sound was high. Then he moved the arm Bill had thought dislocated and grabbed Bill's foot by the toes and transferred his other hand to the heel—and twisted. Pain shot through Bill's ankle. It would have broken if he hadn't fallen, hadn't twisted his body in the direction Staymore was moving his foot, rolling over from his side to his face to his back on the railway corridor floor. In desperation then, Bill kicked out with his free foot at Staymore's hands. His heel hit knuckles. Not very hard. Only grazingly. But the huge priest gasped and dropped Bill's foot. He held his hurt hand close to his face and—suddenly oblivious of Bill—stared at it to the total exclusion of everything else. And then he crammed a podgy finger into his mouth and sucked it and pouted like a huge and horrible travesty of a child.

Bill wriggled back out of reach of the priest. For a second he stared at him sucking his finger there and he felt hatred and not understanding and dread. Then he got fast to his feet.

Staymore's eyes flicked up from his finger at him. They opened a little as if with a surprised sort of sudden understanding. He grunted from deep within his body and, finger forgotten, lumbered quickly up.

But even before the priest's huge bulk was upright once more, Bill had turned and was running.

Running for his life.

With every pounding stride his ankle pained and beneath his feet the floor of the speeding train swayed and shook and juddered as though with malicious intent to make him stumble. But he didn't stumble. Because behind him thundered death in a black priest's robe and that lent grip to his feet. And he ran. Through two first-class Pullmans, white-tableclothed in dainty waiting. Through the gaping grey metal pen of a luggage van with only the sound of his feet to fill it. Into a second-class openplan carriage and half-way through its red-striped emptiness and the feeling that maybe he had got away and then the realisation that there was nowhere to get away to, nowhere but the train to go. Then into a corridor coach. And, even as he wondered with a rebirth of hope if perhaps he could barricade himself behind a toilet door, there was an axe of pain across his spine that seemed to guillotine his head from his shoulders and the floor chopped up in a solid grey wave at his face.

His lips were open onto the grit of the floor and there was a smell like mud and cement in his nose. Right along his back he was paralysed. He tried to lift his head from the cold rattling metal. He got it about four inches up. Then he vomited and his face fell forwards into his sick. Afterwards, he turned his head, resting his cheek on the floor, and felt his fluttering weak gut and the sweat-wet all along his body. He was a little stronger. He was able to hump up a shoulder and squirm over so that he lay on his back.

The Reverend Sullivan Staymore stood looking down at him. The priest's arms hung loose, his hands joined loose in front of him as though in prayer. He was relaxed and serene. In the eerie light from the swirling fog outside his face glistened a phosphorescent grey.

"My dear," he said, "you are trying to avoid me."

Bill said nothing. Whatever the man had done to him, he had practically killed him with a single blow. There wasn't any fighting that kind of force. And now he couldn't run. He could feel some of his strength coming back, but he was too shattered, he knew, even to stand. Sweet Jesus, he didn't want to die! He wondered if he had the strength to drag himself back a little. The toilet was in the communicating bit between carriages. About thirty feet from where he lay. Even if he had the power to get there, the priest would never let him. But, he had to try! Surely his lifelong dream, no, his certainty, that he was destined to get every last good thing from life, was not false, would not die with him here on this filthy floor. He made a huge effort and elbowed himself back. Maybe six inches.

The Reverend Sullivan Staymore looked down on his little effort—and smiled. "Tut!" he said. "Still trying to avoid me!"

Bill continued to drag himself backwards and progressed perhaps another foot.

"You must not try to avoid me."

Bill scrabbled on back.

"We must never run from what the Lord in his infinite wisdom chooses to send."

Bill went on.

"You see, my dear, we are in this world merely to prepare ourselves for the world to come. And all our little trials, our tribulations, are part of this preparation. They come to us from God. They are His gift and must be faced up to, indeed *welcomed,* gladly. Especially pain. Bodily pain. Pain purifies. It is a special, special blessing."

Staymore paused and smiled benignly down at Bill, who was now maybe four feet from him—and struggling on. "I am going to confer this blessing on you now," Staymore said.

Bill looked up from the floor at the grimacing madman. Perhaps it was the sombre light or the sweat running down into his

165

eyes but he couldn't see him very well. All he could tell was that the man was only five feet away and that the toilet was another twenty-five and that if Staymore decided to move, he could be on him in two strides and that there was no conceivable way he could ever reach the toilet in time.

"Wait!" he pleaded desperately.

Staymore stood where he was and continued to smile inanely. Bill's face worked in supplication. He opened his mouth, but no words came out. He had suddenly noticed that the compartment by which he lay had its door open and that if he swung his legs round through ninety degrees and jackknifed his body, he would be inside it and then perhaps could shut the door and somehow wedge himself in there.

"Look . . ." he began to stall, taking the weight of his legs at the base of his spine. "I'm sorry . . ." He measured the distance. "I lost . . ." He tensed himself. ". . . my temper!"

Bill swung his legs into the compartment, flipped over onto his side, pushing his body through . . .

He almost made it.

But Staymore was quick. He took the two strides separating him from the compartment and, before Bill could get fully inside it, smashed forward the door, catching him on the chest—trapping him between the door and the door jamb. The breath slammed from his body, Bill lay on the floor, piniioned as between a pair of giant pliers, helpless. Then, in desperation, he managed to get an arm up and a hand against the edge of the door. He pushed with all the strength he had.

"Silly child," the voice of the priest came down to him.

Bill's face was close to the floor. Staymore's sandalled, grey-socked feet were close to his face. Bill couldn't see more of the man than those feet and about half his black-robed legs. But Bill didn't need to see more to know that the priest was going to kill him. He made a mighty effort to push off the door that held him. Perhaps Staymore was relaxing. It seemed to give a little. Bill made a dart to get back. He did get back a little. Then the door came forward again. And caught him. By the neck.

"Wretch!" the Reverend Sullivan Staymore said above him.

166

"Please!" Bill managed to croak.

He still had a hand against the edge of the door, but it was pressing with throttling force against his windpipe. Blood was throbbing in his temples. There was only red before his eyes. On the other side of the door, his legs and body began to judder and writhe of their own volition. Uncontrollably.

"I am the instrument of the Lord!" declared the priest in a proud and mighty voice. And he leant harder on the sliding door.

The doors of the compartment on British Rail aren't noted for being particularly sharp. But place enough weight behind them, put them to a man's neck, and even their gently curving edge can prove sufficient to part that man from his head. Staymore had enough weight. More than enough. He applied it now.

"Kill him!"

Staymore paused. He looked up along the corridor. A little girl with requiem-black hair was standing close to him, shaking with excitement. She stomped her feet.

"Kill him!" she shrieked once more. "Squash off his head!"

Staymore stood absolutely still for some time while the child danced and gibbered. Then he noticed he was leaning against a compartment door in a careless, rather slovenly way. He let it go and stood upright. There was a commandment about what the child had said. What was it now?

"You've got froth all over your jaw!" the little girl pointed at him, giggling delightedly.

Ah yes! "Thou shalt not kill." He spoke his thought out loud to her.

"But you have. You already have!" And with her giggle become a cackle now she looked down at the corridor floor.

Staymore followed her eyes. To his surprise he saw that there was a young man lying there on the floor at his feet, half in and half out of a compartment. He was lying absolutely still. His face was an extraordinary colour. Blood had come out around his nose. He certainly looked unwell. What could he be doing there? It was all most confusing. Still—there wasn't a sparrow that fell or something but that God didn't know. That was very right and proper. He looked back at the little girl. She was smiling at him. She had odd eyes but rather a nice smile. She held out her hand. He took it. She led him away.

They went off hand-in-hand together down the corridor.

CHAPTER 13

ANN Cross reached up and pulled down the communication cord that would stop the train.

She was too practical a woman to be indignant. If something
bothered her she simply dealt with it till it didn't. And yet—she
was indignant now. Possibly because what bothered her was
something with which she could not deal. Possibly to hide from
herself the fact that she was afraid.

It was outrageous, she thought, quite shocking. When they
got to Dover, she would file a complaint. In this impenetrable
fog, it was nothing less than a scandal that the train should be
moving at all—let alone going at this suicidal speed. Why, it
couldn't be more dangerous!

She tugged once more on the chain. It was dangling now in
her hand. She pulled till it wouldn't come any further down.

It made no difference.

And then her outrage was gone. And a lot of what worked in her mind was gone with it—submerged under a leaden numbness. A sense of knowing it would happen all along, of the inevitability of disaster. She was not surprised the chain hadn't worked, that the train clattered relentlessly on. She knew there was little that could happen now which could surprise her.

But, after a while, the toughness that made her successful in life made her shake off her numbness. It was all very well having "known" the stop-thing wouldn't work, but why get so het up about it? Perhaps it was disconnected, never intended to work anyhow; perhaps it was simply out of order; perhaps . . .

She noticed the doctor staring at her. Damn him! He must have been watching her since the moment she got up to pull the cord.

"Well?" she demanded of him.

"Well what?"

"Why didn't it work, then?"

"What?"

"The chain—you fool."

"I've no idea," he replied.

"No, you wouldn't, would you?" She paused, then began to think aloud: "Well . . . I doubt those chains can break. They probably go in one strip all the way through to the driver, so he must—"

"Has it occurred to you that there may not be a driver?" Dr. Latimer interrupted her.

People who tell you what you don't want to hear are not loved. And when they identify in your mind with the man you despised above all others, they become less lovely still. For a heartbeat or two, Ann Cross gaped at the man opposite. Then her controlled face tore apart in a snarl and the hands that had been drumming restlessly in her lap balled up into claws.

"You bloody, bloody fool!" She stabbed the words at him.

Dr. Latimer shrugged. "Think about it," he suggested calmly; then turned and stared in his habitual bland way into the corridor—and beyond, into the faceless, impenetrable fog.

Ann Cross thought about it, all right. But her "it" was not what he meant. It was the joy, the unimaginable joy, she would take in destroying Dr. Robert Latimer—the man who reminded her not only of her father but now of all the fools she had trampled on over the years. She thought of some horrible things to do to him and it brought a moment's relief from the other thoughts that were crowding oppressively in on her brain. But only a moment's. There were questions too important to be put aside. None more so than the basic—what was going on? It was no good trying to persuade herself that this weather, those things she had seen outside were capable of normal explanation. No. It was as if the whole train had slipped out of the normal universe into . . . what? Something—somewhere—else. From a memory of a near-forgotten conversation, the words "a different continuum" came into her mind. But they didn't help her. She didn't know what they meant.

"You can't have a train without a driver!" she told Dr. Latimer.

"No," he agreed, turning his eyes from the dark and empty corridor to her face.

"I mean, it would be totally out of control."

"Yes, it would."

"It isn't possible!"

"No," he agreed once more, his expressionless face turning to the window, "but, then—is any of this?"

Suddenly, Ann Cross only knew or cared about one thing. She had to get out of this compartment.

It seemed days she had been here. No. Just since Victoria Station. God, that was a long, long way away. Maybe it wasn't, though. Maybe it was only an hour. All she knew was, she had to get out. She picked up her handbag, got ready to stand, looked out into the corridor—and all the fear she had suppressed and pushed down deep within her over seventeen years sprang free.

She remained in her seat. Locked there. By terror. Anything could be waiting out there. Not a person had been by since the journey began. Suppose the young man had been right—there *was* no one else on the train? And what had happened to him and the priest and the little girl? They had all been gone a long time now. In an ice-water-cold shock of insight, she saw that they would not be coming back. Oh no, she wouldn't commit herself to that corridor! Would not give whatever was out there the chance to take her also; would not go out and get lost and never find her way back. No! She would sit here forever if need be, rather than step out into that darkness. Here, here in the light she was safe.

You're nuts!

The rational part of Ann's mind screamed at her. You're thinking just like your parents—like *them*. But then that part of her mind began to loose its hold—and besides, she realised, she didn't really want to go anywhere now anyway.

"If we want an explanation for what we see, we must look for it elsewhere than in the obvious," Dr. Latimer said thoughtfully.

Ann focused on him. He was staring out into the corridor in his usual blank way. But then, all of a sudden, his face began to acquire expression. The expression spread across his face, crumbling its blankness, forcing open his mouth. The expression was shock. Ann followed his gaze. Out into the corridor. To the greyness beyond it. The fog—the fog was breaking up. It was fragmenting, moving back to left and right as if from some central point. A valley was forming through it. She could see a landscape between the two receding walls of the fog.

It was a landscape that couldn't exist in this world.

She saw a plain. It went away to distance. It was rock, black rock. In patches slimy earth clung to it like huge flayed scabs of flesh in clumsy graft to bone. Little grew on the earth, except, occasionally, faint clots of fungus. They looked like suppurating brain burst through the cranium of a charred and shaven skull.

"Jesus!" Ann Cross whispered and she didn't know that she had. It was as near to a prayer as she would get in her life.

There was a river now. A speckling froth of scum more nearly solid than fluid, like a sludge of Auschwitz-incinerated ash. Steam rose off it, writhed a snake-slimed phosphorescent brown. Ann stared at it all in terror, disbelief. Then, abruptly, the two sides of fog which had parted like curtains on the scene, hurtled together again and clashed and blended, spun off tentacles of mist that twined till all were one once more and fog alone was all there was to see.

Stunned, Ann turned towards Latimer. He didn't look calm now. His face was the decomposing grey of the river. As he swivelled his eyes across to hers, there was a gleam in them and he grinned an alligator grin.

"Strontium 90! Has to be!" he exclaimed with an enthusiasm she was too dazed to notice. He looked at her as if hungry for some reply. But she was hollow. Had only half-heard and did not understand what he said.

"It will mutate!" he went on. "Will distort and pervert in endless permutations!" His manner was nervous, pecky. He was thrusting forwards his face as he talked now in jerks like a crow.

Suddenly, Ann thought she understood him. Yes. Oh God, yes. And he was right! He had to be. It was the only thing which could explain what she'd seen out there. Her voice was dead as she looked into his gleaming eyes and said it.

"They dropped the bomb."

For a second it was like she'd hit him in the stomach. He bent sharply forward, as if to bob his head on his knees, then straightened up and flopped back against his seat. He gave a whoop of laughter, began to cackle insanely. My God, she thought, hating him, he's mad. She had never known anything less funny than what she had seen out there in her life. Nor could she in that moment imagine any more painful way than radiation sickness to die. And yet, she thought, with a sudden gush of hope, if they *had* dropped the bomb, if that horror out there had been caused by radioactivity, it would have been of such intensity that she herself must already, by now, be destroyed. Of course! It couldn't be the Third World War. The world wasn't ending yet after all. But then she thought—what did it matter if the world were ending or not, as long as she herself were to die? God, why had she thought that? She wasn't in any danger. No? Then what did that apocalyptic landscape mean? She was glad the fog curtained it at least . . . oh, it was hard to think. The man-so-like-her-father's manic laughter was shredding up her brain.

"Shut up!" she screamed at him.

But Dr. Latimer was not used to laughing and, having begun, found it difficult to stop. His laughter grew high, hysterical, more and more uncontrolled. Ann Cross watched him. She wanted to kill him. She wished she could take a shotgun and blow that grimacing face to fragments all over the seat behind it. If she had some sort of weapon, she really could get him, she realised with a sudden thrill. There was no one here to know but herself and him!

And the scruffy man.

All at once she noticed him. He had been there asleep so long it was like he was part of the fixtures. God Almighty! Some of her fear-born anger transferred its target to him. We could be at war, could have entered some other dimension! It may be the end of the world—but that little punk sleeps through it all. Not even the bone-shaking speed of the train, the lunatic cackling of the doctor beside him, disturbed his sleep. It was high time she changed that, Ann thought—and she pulled back her foot to kick the dormant man's knee.

The Reverend Sullivan Staymore walked into the compartment.

Ann translated the movement of her foot into crossing her legs. The priest went past her to his seat. She studied him. His expression was serene and placid—that of a man enjoying a concert of restful music. The little girl came in after him. She looked indrawn. Excited but contained.

"Have a good laugh, Daddy," she said as she went by her father.

Then, rather than resume her place beside Ann, she went and sat by the window opposite the priest. She settled there gazing at him. And her expression was the pride of ownership of a young child who had just gained possession of a long-coveted, brand-new doll.

For a moment Ann experienced a strange relief that they had returned. But then she saw they also were mad. Quite mad, she thought. Everyone here is. Insane. She had to get out of this! Right away. She snatched her face towards the corridor. It filled

174

her with dread. She knew she dare not move. She was trapped. Oh God! Where was the young man? Maybe he could help her. But wait—something was . . . different. Oh. The father-man had stopped laughing. He looked like it had drained him of the little life he had. His face was drawn in, eyes were void. He was a mummy.

"Where's the man who was sitting where you are?" Ann snapped at Felicity.

The little girl slowly turned her head. She beamed her cloud-white eyes on Ann then turned back again to watch the priest. Gloating. Silent.

Ann didn't waste time on the lunatic child. She addressed Staymore. Suddenly this mattered to her. "When you were out in the corridor," she asked, wondering if her voice was normal, "you didn't see the man who sits opposite you, did you, Father?" And then she thought—*father!* Whose father? The word stayed in her brain, did damage there.

Staymore slowly turned his face in her direction. He looked at her. But maybe he didn't see her or thought she was a congregation. He parted his hands and held them, sweating palms outwards, by his shoulders as if bestowing a blessing. Or starting to preach.

"I looked," he intoned, "and behold, a pale horse: and his name that sat on him was Death, and Hell followed with him."

Felicity twittered in ecstasy.

Beneath their compartment was a sound like *clackety-clack*.

"You're bloody mad!" Ann Cross told Staymore. "Mad. And so are you and you!" She spat at Felicity and her father.

But neither of them took any notice of her. And the priest merely smiled benignly and said in the gentle voice of one who could forgive any betrayal: "I know thy works, that thou hast a name that thou livest, and art dead."

At which point, it all got too much for Ann Cross, granite woman that she was, and she huddled in her corner of the shaking rattling compartment and for the first time since she was thirteen, she began to cry.

CHAPTER 14

THERE was light.

Red. A spider thread of it. It put out other threads. The skeletal outline of a tiny tree. It waved, grew thicker. Its trunk grew thicker at the base; its branches melted down to join into its trunk. It was a triangle. No. A rectangle. No, a hand-drawn circle wavy round the edges. It was alive. It was pulsing, spinning off orange and yellow and white whorls of light around its perimeter like the sun. It was growing stronger, reaching out into blackness all around it and lighting it till it revealed that there were other throbbing colours where once had been the dark.

There was sound.

Soft. But coming louder. A scratching. Feet of mice on membrane. Fluttery, quick. A bang-bang-banging door blown back and forth in distance by the wind. It steadied, loudened, neared.

It was a boulder bouncing on a park-size kettle-drum. Reaching out to fill the universe with throb of sound, filling, just like the light it beat to, synchronized itself to; throbbing, flashing, throbbing out—

Pain.

In the blood-whorls reeling before his eyes, in the heart-beat smashing against his brain.

Bill Armstrong had come back from death.

He came not like Lazarus, in joy from death so final that his body had gotten to rot in the tomb. He came reluctantly in agony from death's brink by asphyxiation. Called back unwillingly by Felicity Latimer, who had startled his murderer into relaxing his hold—by telling him to kill.

Bill Armstrong did not want to live. The pain was far too much. All above his shoulders was a flayed and torn and blood-blistered weal of agony where his throat and head no longer had any right to be. That agony alone should have been enough to kill him. It hadn't. But it made him desperately want to die and now, with what little will he had, he fought against life, tried to return to oblivion, feebly fought the horror of returning consciousness.

He lost. Man seldom dies merely by wanting to.

Bill lay on the floor on his face as the priest had left him and he cried like a child with a sense of the unfairness of it all and his helplessness. And all the while the circulation burned its way back through his neck to his head and fiery maggots of pain crawled round and round in his skull.

Time passed.

Instinct made him try to pick himself up. He hunched onto his elbows, got a knee towards them, pushed up with his hands. He knelt on the floor, leaning on his straightened arms, but they started to tremble uncontrollably and weren't able to take his weight and he fell back into a half-sitting position against the jamb of the sliding door. Like a corpse he sat there, lolling loosely with the shake of the train. After a little he undertook to stand. It should have been a simple operation, but he was desperately weakened: his legs seemed a long way away from him and did not answer his brain. They trembled, would not stay where he placed them. When he finally got some weight on them, they crumpled beneath him and he nearly pitched back onto his face on the floor. As it was, however, he caught against the door. And not long after that he was trying to stand again.

It was some time before he finally succeeded. Even then he had to hold for support to the side of the door.

Bill stood. He looked vacantly down the empty long corridor, down the windows of the rushing, eternal fog. Bill Armstrong was broken. He reached, got a grip on the window rail across the corridor from him and, holding heavily to it, began to shamble away.

Like a badly hurt child limping home to its mother, he went unthinking back towards his compartment.

CHAPTER 15

THE sweat that the body excretes in fear is sour and salty and has a particularly acrid smell. The compartment reeked of that smell now. But as Bill Armstrong slowly and weakly pulled back the sliding door and came in, he was too numbed to notice it.

There was much he did not notice: the way the woman gaped up at him with a famished look of hope that changed to dismay as she perceived his void expression, lacerated neck; the priest's silently working lips, his gaze set into distance; the flaring-eyed surprise of the little girl.

"Golly," Felicity exclaimed, "a zombie!"

But Bill did not hear that, nor appear to see that she was in his place as he stepped on uncertain legs past Ann Cross and half-fell onto the seat beside her. He stared down at the floor for a moment or two and then his forehead creased with pain and his eyes heavily closed. At no time had he even glanced in the direction of the Reverend Sullivan Staymore.

Propelled perhaps by the movement of the train, certainly without anyone touching it, the sliding door that Bill Armstrong had left open behind him suddenly clunked shut.

Bill's eyes opened. For a second they were lucid and clear and afraid. Nervously, he looked to right and left and, doing so, noticed his briefcase on the floor by where he had previously sat. He stared at it a second. Then he fumbled down past Felicity Latimer's legs and scooped it up. He held it against his chest and folded his arms around it and hugged it to him. Felicity watched him as he did this and grinned.

"Careful you don't drop it!" she mocked.

But the momentary clearness had left Bill Armstrong's eyes. Once again he stared dazedly in front of him and did not reply.

"What have you done to your neck?" Ann Cross asked him sharply in a voice that trembled near hysteria.

Bill turned his head towards her.

"He caught it in a door!" Felicity Latimer twittered.

"Yes," Bill agreed and turned away.

"*Do* something!" Ann rounded on Dr. Latimer.

He stared at her with sockets as blank as a skeleton's gazing up from a coffin.

"You're a doctor, aren't you? Help him!" She snatched across at him and her hand clamped onto his thigh just above the knee and the strong, well-manicured finger-nails of her hand went into his flesh.

He jerked away from her hand. Seeing him move was like watching an electric current put to the nerve ends of a corpse. His face was still without colour and no animation came to it as he spoke:

"You keep expecting something to be done. You fail to appreciate that there is nothing—*nothing*—that any of us can do." But then he got up and reached up onto the rack above him and brought down his doctor's bag. He sat with it on his knee and looked across at Ann. She stared savagely back at him. A glint of what may have been amusement flickered deep in his eyes. He opened the bag.

"Lo!" the Reverend Sullivan Staymore boomed out, loud and sudden, "there was a great earthquake."

Everyone in the compartment looked at him. He saw none of them. "And the sun," he went on, "became black as sackcloth of hair, and the moon became as blood."

Staymore paused. Dr. Latimer reached into his bag and took out a hypodermic. "Where would you like me to begin?" he asked Ann dryly.

"With yourself!" she snarled at him. And then Staymore was speaking again:

"The stars of heaven fell unto the earth, even as a fig tree casteth her untimely figs, when she is shaken of a mighty wind. And the heaven departed as a scroll when it is rolled together."

Dr. Latimer filled the hypodermic from an ampoule. He examined the level of fluid inside it; held the needle up, depressed the plunger and expelled air from inside the syringe.

"And every man hid themselves in the dens and in the rocks of the mountains; and said to them, Fall on us, and hide us from the wrath of him that sitteth on the throne, and from the wrath of the Lamb!"

Staymore had reached a crescendo. He paused. Then, gazing in front of him with the fervour of divine revelation, he preached:

"Mary had a little lamb. Its fleece was white as snow. And everywhere that Mary went, the lamb was sure to go!"

Felicity whooped with laughter. As from a distance, Staymore noticed her, smiled on her benignly. Dr. Latimer sat looking at the two of them, syringe, needle upwards in his hand. Felicity recovered from her laughter. She looked across at her father and a white ice beamed from her eyes.

"It won't be long now, Daddy," she told him.

Then she looked maternally over at Staymore once again and parted her pale lips and smiled. Still smiling, she got up from her place and stepped across to him and climbed up onto his lap. He accepted her there without surprise or reaction, as if it were a thing he had been doing for her all her life. She sat with her back to him and he bounced his leg up and down and jogged her, as one would a tiny child. Like this, in silence, they looked out the window together.

And then everyone else in the compartment looked out also. They were coming alongside another train.

They had sensed it before they had seen it. Perhaps because of some alteration in the sound their own train was making—its clatter not fading into open space and fog, but being bounced back from a solid object close at hand. Certainly some seconds before they saw the train, they knew it was there. And then it came into vision. Slowly. Less than ten yards away and running parallel to them and they were overtaking it. Steadily, inexorably, their compartment moved down the length of the other train. And the fog seemed to have cleared, for they could see across and into it clearly.

There were people in the other train.

People. In the compartments, reading, talking, sleeping, moving up and down in the corridors. They were eating in the Pullman cars, standing gazing out of the windows of the corridors and just sitting and doing absolutely nothing as most people on trains usually do. They were very normal, very near—and to those who watched them they were an unobtainable other world away.

Their compartment had slowly passed several on the neighbouring train before Ann Cross unfroze. Then she sprang up and jumped to the window and began to wave. There was another compartment directly opposite and a man in it was leaning on an elbow, looking pensively out of his window. He was staring straight towards Ann and he seemed almost near enough to touch. She waved at him.

"Hey!" she shouted as their compartments slowly crossed.

He did not notice her.

Ann tried to pull back the sliding window then. She wrenched and tugged at it desperately. She broke a finger-nail. She went on tugging. But the window wouldn't budge. She beat on the glass with her fists. She waved her arms wildly, frantically shouted at the top of her voice towards the other train.

"*Hey!* You all there, hey, look!"

"They cannot hear you," Dr. Latimer said, with a faint smile.

Felicity grinned. "Try shouting. Go on!"

"*Help* me!" Ann Cross screamed.

She spun away from the window and flung herself against the sliding door of the compartment and heaved on it. But something had caused it to jam. Despite her utmost efforts, it did not move in the least degree.

"Stuck?" Dr. Latimer inquired solicitously.

"You've got to pull harder," Felicity twittered. "Try again!"

Ann did try. She tried with all the strength she had, but it availed her not at all. Finally, panting, swearing, sweating, she fell back beaten into her seat. Irredeemably cut off from it, she watched the nice full normal train go by. There were so many people on it, so many looking in their direction, yet in not one of their eyes was there any sign they had seen them at all.

Now the final length of the other train's engine slid past into greyness like a ship sinking down to the silence of the sea. And the fog came back.

Clack.

The snap of a metal bolt the length of a railway train shooting home to its socket.

It was the last sound they heard from outside.

From that moment, though the train still palpably moved and shook and juddered beneath and around them, it did so in silence. There was no sound of wheels, no sound of engines, no sound of metal, none of wind. There was the breathing of frightened people and that of a man asleep. There was the nervous twitter of a little girl.

"We must be there!" Felicity Latimer gasped.

And perfectly on cue, exactly as she said it, the light, such light as there was outside the window, went out. Just like that. As if someone had flicked a switch and extinguished it. Where once had been grey fog was now blackness. Total and unrelieved. A blackness so intense it hurt the eyes—and which you knew no light would ever penetrate.

"We in a tunnel, are we?"

The scruffy man had woken. He had yawned and stretched—and seen the blackness outside. Now, with growing dismay, he took in the rest of his surroundings. They were terrifyingly weird. The little girl was sitting next to him, staring at him strangely from the lap of the priest. He turned round to the man on his other side. Incredibly, he was holding a naked hypodermic needle. The man opposite looked like someone had tried to chop his head off with a club and the woman beside him, who had been so elegant at the start of the journey—her hair was awry and through her makeup her face was streaked with sweat and tears. The expression of everyone of them was staring-eyed and strange. Lord, they were appalling! They made his flesh crawl. For a moment he sat there in shock. Then he got up quickly and went to the compartment door. But he found he could not open it. He heaved on it. As he did so, he could feel eyes on his back, watching as he could not open the door.

"Has someone locked this or something?" he asked, turning round.

The woman began to cackle like a witch. The little girl stared stone into his eyes. But that was all the reaction his question had.

He sat down. There wasn't anything else to do.

"You aren't meant to be here!" Felicity Latimer said.

The scruffy man wished he weren't. And if he could find out how to open the door he wouldn't be, either! He addressed himself to the doctor. He tried to make his voice sound casual and light-hearted.

"There isn't some trick to opening that I should know, is there?" he asked, nodding towards the door.

Dr. Latimer looked at him with a face which said nothing.

The man frowned. He stared back at Latimer, then down at the bare needle in his hand. "Hey," he said, "don't you think you ought to put that away?"

The doctor showed no sign of having heard. Exasperated, the scruffy man turned away to Felicity as being the only person

184

there who had so far acknowledged his existence. He nodded towards her father. "He all right?" he asked quietly.

"Everyone here is all wrong!" She smiled.

Staymore suddenly spoke. There was sorrow in his voice. "Babylon the great is fallen, is fallen," he said, "for all nations have drunk of the wine of the wrath of her fornication."

"Bounce me!" Felicity Latimer pouted.

Obediently, Staymore began to bounce her up and down on his knee. She smiled complacently and took one of his hands and began to pull and play with his oblate fingers.

The scruffy man was scared. This was all some ugly nightmare. He turned his attention to Ann. He tried to sound normal as he said: "Isn't this rather a long tunnel we're in?" He waited for a reply but she seemed lost somewhere deep inside herself. He knew he had to keep talking, though. As long as he did, maybe this whole thing would stay in some sort of reach of sanity. For he had just noticed something else—and it wasn't possible. The train was moving. But it wasn't making a sound.

He would try talking to the man opposite. Maybe he'd notice him. Yes! But the scruffy man's voice quavered as he said: "Umm, is—is—it just my ears? I can't hear much noise from the engine."

"That is because you are such a noisy, nasty little man."

It was the doctor beside him. As he turned his head to face him, the scruffy man felt a sharp jab in his arm. Automatically he jerked away from it, but he found his arm was being held. He looked down. The hypodermic needle was sticking through his jacket into his flesh. The contents of the syringe had entered his vein. It wasn't possible. He was stunned. The doctor withdrew the needle.

"Now you will be quiet," he said.

"About time!" said the woman opposite.

"Have you killed him, Daddy? Have you killed him?" the child demanded with obscene and terrifying eagerness.

But even as the scruffy man turned his stunned face back towards the doctor and strained to catch his reply, a great heavy water washed over him and took away his consciousness and he never heard what was said.

"Wouldn't you like to know!" Dr. Latimer sneered at his daughter—and neatly replaced the syringe in his bag.

"As the vessels of a potter shall they be broken to shivers," Staymore said.

"Lousy spoil-sport!" Felicity sneered back at her father.

And at that moment, all by itself, the compartment door slid back.

It opened fully. Stayed in position. Fixedly. They stared in silence at that open door. And then Felicity Latimer whispered: "This is it!"

It was.

From the black silent void of the corridor that gaped at them through the open door came a sound. It was a gentle sound. Faint, as if from distance. But getting nearer. It was a tinkling, as of many tiny bells—not unlike those that mountain-grazing animals in Switzerland wear round their necks, except that these were many, many tiny bells all building into a single sound the way of hiving bees. And as the sound got nearer, it became more like the harnessed hum of a dynamo—pulsing off force as it came.

The sound stayed soft, but it came closer, and out of the blackness of the corridor there came with the sound a faint and only slightly phosphorescing light. Magenta light.

The light and sound got nearer.

Felicity Latimer jumped off the knee of the priest. She ran her hands over her dress. She turned to the window. The blackness outside made it a mirror and, watching herself in it, she smoothed out her long dark hair. She was humming a little tune to herself, humming with excitement. She spun round from the window.

"It's Him!" she exclaimed to Staymore. And then, radiant and blooming and with all the eagerness of a mistress going to her lover, she skipped out into the passage towards the pulse of magenta light.

They could hear her humming happily as she went down the

186

corridor. The light was a little brighter. Felicity sounded like she was about to sing.

Then they heard her scream.

In agony. A lung-bursting howl of pain and horror. Long and high—and quite suddenly shorn off.

The magenta light was a little brighter. The dynamo tinkle of bells a little nearer.

Ann Cross spun round at Bill Armstrong. She clutched his arm and pleaded: "Help. Help *me!*" But her words had no effect and she let his arm go and a tremble ran through her whole body and softly she began to mutter and sob and chuckle to herself.

Dr. Robert Latimer watched and he was suddenly filled with awareness of life, of its value and wonder, and for the first time in his existence he very much wanted to live. But he realised he was a little late.

Bill Armstrong looked at the hysterical woman also. There was something he had once wanted from her. Yes. He had a jumbled sense that there was a thing he had to do. He shuffled up the seat a little towards her; with effort stretched out a hand. But he didn't know what to do with it—and then all his weak mind could think was:

HELL.

EPILOGUE

At eleven fifty-two on Friday, the twenty-fourth of September, 1971, the Golden Arrow got into Dover Station much as usual. It was a blustery autumn day with white clouds chipping quickly across a bracing high blue sky. The train was two minutes late but none of its passengers seemed particularly worried by that as they climbed down out of their carriages and crowded along the platform.

In a first-class carriage, a scruffy man awoke with a throbbing head and a stiffness in his arm—though his head hurt too much for him to notice it. He was alone in a compartment and, as he groggily came to consciousness, could not for a time make out what he was doing there. Then he remembered, miserably, that he had caught the wrong train from London. He must have slept all the way. God, he felt ill. He had a vague memory of a nightmare. Swearing never to drink again, he put it from his mind and got to his feet. He fumbled with the door and stumbled down onto the breezy platform. He did not notice the luggage in the racks he left behind.

The station foreman found it later, when combing, as he always did, through the empty train.

He was surprised. Never before had he seen so much luggage abandoned in one place—all those expensive-looking cases, the doctor's bag, the briefcase right there on the seat. It was most unusual. He took it all into the station to where they kept lost property and, hoping to find some identification inside it, opened the briefcase.

What he saw amazed him. Incredulous, he gazed into the open case. Heck, he thought, what sort of guy could get off and leave *that* behind? He'd never seen that much cash in his life. It was all in old fives, used and impossible to trace. For a moment a dishonest thought went through his mind—but he beat it down. As a matter of record, he began to count the money.

It took him quite a long time. Half-way through, he forgot where he'd got to and had to start again. But finally he had it. It staggered him. He was dazed. He shook his head. Where on earth, he wondered, could anybody be going to that they wouldn't need two thousand, two hundred pounds?